A Perfect Fit

DiCarlo Brides Book 1
Love in Juniper Ridge

OTHER WORKS BY HEATHER TULLIS

The DiCarlo Brides
SEALed with Love
Reclaiming his Bride
Family Matters
Wild Hearts
The Last Bride
Getting Her Groom

Other Juniper Ridge novels
Homecoming
Carver Ranch series
Second Chances
Identity
Safe Haven

In the Garden
Hello Again
First Crush
Not in The Plans
Last Chance

Echo Ridge Anthologies
Christmas Kisses
Kisses Between the Lines
Silver Screen Kisses
Second Chance Kisses
Ice Cream Kisses

HEATHER TULLIS

A Perfect Fit

DiCarlo Brides Book 1
Love in Juniper Ridge

Published by Jelly Bean Press, PO Box 548 Osawatomie, KS 66064

ISBN: 978-1-63034-075-9

Cover design © 2018 by Heather Justesen

Front cover image Deposit Photo #35418837 Armina-Udovenko

Back Cover image Adobe Stock Photo #35836729 Veneratio

CAST OF CHARACTERS

Camellia DiCarlo (Cami)—Oldest of George DiCarlo's daughters, born to his wife, head of guest services.

Sage Parker—Second eldest, head of the resort Spa. Born to Darla Parker.

Rosemary Keogh—Third eldest, born to Wanda Keogh, head of resort food services.

Lantana DiCarlo (Lana)—Fourth eldest, second daughter by George's wife, hotel manager.

Delphinium Gifford (Delphi)—Fifth eldest daughter by Zelda Gifford, head of resort events.

Jonquil Chestnut—Sixth eldest daughter by Trudy Chestnut, head of the resort floral center.

Vince Talmadge—Landscape architect, best friend of Jeremy and Gage.

Jeremy Litster—Local photographer, best friend of Vince and Gage.

Gage Mathews—Head of Deer Mountain, the local ski resort. Best friend to Vince and Jeremy.

Harrison Forest—Older half-brother to Sage by another father. Head of hotel HR.

Blake Bahlmann—Regional manager of DiCarlo Resorts, stationed out of the Juniper Ridge resort.

Joel Watts—Former Navy SEAL, head of hotel security.

"They're beautiful." She greeted Wesson, rubbed the soft fur around the dog's bear-like head and giggled when a huge tongue lathered slobber all over her lower arm. The dog jumped up on back legs, propping enormous paws on Cami's shoulders.

"Hold on there, girl." Vince took hold of the dog's collar and pulled her off when Cami took two steps back to keep from falling over. "Sorry. They're still puppies, despite their size, and I haven't had much time to train them this spring."

Not at all put off, Cami smiled, then reached out a hand to rub Smith's face—this time keeping her distance better. "It's fine. I love dogs, but I'm not home enough to keep any of my own. They look almost like Akitas, except the ears."

Vince smiled in surprise. "Part Akita, yes, and part Bullmastiff. Sweet as sugar and not done growing yet." He gave both dogs a good rub, and with a few hand signs, had them sitting on their haunches, quivering with excitement. Then he introduced Sage and Cami to Gage.

"I'm not sure why you were willing to spend time with this joker," Gage said when he held Cami's hand. "But I guess I can't complain, considering."

"Back off, Matthews, this one's all mine." Vince's warm hand enveloped Cami's free one.

The declaration caught Cami by surprise, left her torn between irritation and amusement. For the day, she opted for amusement.

Gage released her. "So noted. It's a pleasure to meet you, anyway." He turned to Sage. "And if the rest of the sisters are as pretty as you two are, our community owes your father a great debt of gratitude." He took her hand and lifted it to his lips.

"You're a smooth one, aren't you?" Sage asked, appearing amused.

His lips quirked. "I try. Do I succeed?"

"I'll let you know." Sage glanced down the street to the oncoming horde of young ones. "Do you have family in the parade?"

Vince answered, "My niece. She's been talking, planning and decorating for weeks. Expect something as spectacular as Barnum and Bailey when she pedals by."

"You don't have any kids or nieces in it?" Cami asked Gage.

"Nope, no kids and no nieces and nephews here." His smile flashed. "I prefer it that way, but the Talmadges always drag me to join them for stuff like this. I guess I'm a glutton for punishment."

Conversation shifted to the kids and Cami studied the crowd. She'd expected two or three dozen kids on bikes or tricycles with a few streamers in red, white and blue. The number of entries was far more than she'd anticipated, though the decorations weren't impressive. A few young girls in matching leotards tried twirling their batons in sync, and failed; boys in top hats and colonial costumes walked by; and the crowds of watchers grew.

Vince's niece, Hannah, rode by on her bike, a red wagon towed behind. Flags erupted from her handlebars, patriotic streamers and metallic ribbons fluttered in the breeze. The wagon held a large, seated teddy bear wearing a dust cap with a flag draped over the wagon and several inches below the sides. A sign touted Betsy Ross's patriotism as she sewed the first flag.

Putting two fingers in her mouth, Cami whistled long and loud for the little girl with brown pigtails. "Go, Hannah!"

Hannah grinned like she couldn't stop.

Cami had always been proud to be from Chicago, of the city's wonders, sounds and excitement. She'd been pleased to know everyone of note, to have contacts everywhere, to get hotel guests exactly what they needed, especially if said needs took some serious wheedling. She'd never realized how much she missed out on, though, living in a city with so many people who were focused on number one. Hotel guests were, by definition, self-absorbed. They weren't part of the community, the history, the area. This was different. This was community.

When the youngsters finished, Hannah rode over on her bike and put up the kickstand, beaming as she accepted hugs and compliments.

"I love the decorations, kiddo," Vince said as Hannah wrapped her arms around his waist. He hauled her up for a bear hug.

"Thanks. You liked it, even though I didn't use your idea of purple mountains majesty?"

"Of course. How could I not?" He tipped his forehead against hers. "Your idea was better."

She giggled again and he set her down, then introduced her to Cami and Sage.

"Is that your real name?" Hannah asked. "I thought you were all supposed to be flowers."

"My name is actually Camellia, but it's a mouthful, don't you think? Not like Hannah which is so pretty." The girl was adorable.

"I like Camellia. Did you like my bike?"

"It is awesome. Definitely the best one out there." Cami

could say that in good conscience, since it was true. "I bet you had to do a lot of research."

"Yeah. Usually they show the flag with a circle of stars, but you know they used to put them in squares and other shapes too." The girl was off and chattering and only stopped when her mom pulled her away ten minutes later to grab some dinner in the park.

"Thanks for being so patient with her," Vince said after they'd cleaned up their things and headed into the fray. He held tightly to his dogs' leashes.

"It's no problem. She's a sweetheart." A huge tent covered a stage and chairs and a mediocre country band was already in full swing when Vince's group arrived. "Interesting blend of music styles," Cami commented when the band switched to a rendition of Bon Jovi's "It's My Life" with a heavy western twang.

"What can we say? We're a colorful people. Are you hungry?" Vince asked.

"Oh, yeah. Cami wouldn't let me near the kitchen—she was anxious about whatever food would be available here," Sage said.

"It's our responsibility to support the locals, which means filling up from the food booths," Cami justified.

"I like your line of thinking, and while you're at it, I think there are a few changes you ought to make to the landscaping at your place," Vince said with a twinkle in his eye.

Cami elbowed him playfully and he shifted away before she made contact, laughing. "Let's focus on dinner for now, okay?" she said. "I'm starving."

They wandered through the thoroughfare, then headed back, stopping at a Navajo taco booth for dinner. While they waited in the long line, Joel, the security guy from the hotel whom they'd met during their tour, approached them. "How are you all doing tonight?"

Though she wasn't interested herself, Cami couldn't help but notice the warm look Sage gave him. Joel was at least six-foot-four, shaved bald, and was easily 250 pounds of solid muscle—not surprising once she learned he was a former Navy SEAL. Even smiling, he could be one intimidating guy.

"We're great. Are you here by yourself today?" Sage asked him.

Joel's lips curved. "Not anymore. At least not if you don't mind me crashing your party." Though the words were uncertain, his attitude wasn't. He fully intended to join them, and if Sage's answering smile was anything to go by, she didn't mind in the least.

"The more the merrier," Vince said. "I don't think we've met. I'm Vince Talmadge." He and his friends went through the round of introductions and Joel settled into line with them.

They rejoined the family, and Cami was happy to meet Jeremy, Vince's other best friend. He'd been busy snapping photos of happy children during the parade. He had a brunette on his arm, Krissa, who claimed to be just a friend, but the way she clung to him sent a different message.

When Krissa jumped up to greet a couple of friends, Sage looked at Jeremy, whose gaze had been following his date. "She's not the one, you know."

Surprise filled his face. "Who says I'm looking for the right woman? I enjoy my single life."

Sage's brows lifted. "Yeah. You keep saying that, but the woman you'll marry is just around the corner." She tipped her head a little, studying him, making him squirm a little.

Joel shifted a little closer to Sage, his gaze darting around the park. He didn't seem to think the comment weird at all.

Cami was surprised by Sage's comment. She chuckled, trying to wave away the odd behavior—what was with this woman, anyway? "She's making all kinds of interesting predictions today. I wouldn't take all that woo-woo stuff too seriously."

A flash of hurt crossed Sage's face before it disappeared. "Obviously I'm just joking with you. No one can know stuff like that." She turned back to talk with Joel as if to shut the rest of them out, leaving Cami to feel guilty about the comment.

There was a moment of silence before Hannah ran over to cajole Vince into dancing with her. Almost as one, the group stood and headed for the music tent.

CHAPTER 11

When they had danced a few songs to the Mexican Banda group that had taken over while they ate, Vince led Cami to the edge of the dance floor where the others were sitting. "So, there's a balloon launch in the morning. Either of you ever been up before?" he asked both Cami and Sage.

"I have. It was cool stuff. I did it once in high school." Sage looked at Cami. "Dad happened to visit the right weekend, and paid for the two of us to go up. Of course he spent the time pointing out different kinds of plants and trees and lecturing me on erosion."

Cami chuckled, despite the twinge of pain and sadness the comment brought up. "Sounds like him. I wish I could say I had a turn, but alas, my timing must have stunk."

"You want to? I'm launching a balloon in the morning, I can take on an extra couple of people," Vince suggested.

Cami grinned at the thought. "What do you think?" she asked Sage, hoping she'd say no thanks.

"I think you totally ought to go. One trip was fun, but I'm better off with my feet on the ground, thanks." She rubbed her stomach and grimaced. "I didn't mention that I felt more than a little queasy by the time the balloon landed again. I guess I wasn't meant to fly."

"So you want to come alone?" Vince asked Cami.

She ought to say no, but it wasn't like anything untoward was going to happen in an air balloon. Spending the evening with him surrounded by family and friends cured her lingering wariness. She was starting to think he was just what he appeared to be—even if he had surprising facets. Ballooning. Huh. "It sounds like fun. I don't get motion sickness, so I should be fine."

"Wish I could go up with you," Jeremy said. "But I'll be taking pictures on the ground for the local magazine."

"And they'll be spectacular, since you'll know what to expect," Krissa said with a giggle.

He whispered something in her ear, making her giggle more.

"And I'm running the mountain bike race in the morning," Gage said to Sage. "If you have some time, come over to Deer Mountain and I'll show you around." He mentioned a major ski resort in the area.

"Deer Mountain? You work over there?" Cami asked. She still needed to make some contacts in that direction.

"Yeah. I understand you're the one who hooks guests up with last-minute passes and stuff." Gage brushed off a fly buzzing past his face. "If so, I'm the one you need to speak with."

"That's my department. What can you do for me?"

They spent twenty minutes discussing summer events, ski packages, and activities organized by the ski resort year round. She wished she'd brought a notebook.

"Swing by on Monday and we'll go over it in more detail, see if we can work out a package deal," he suggested.

"I'll do that. About ten work for you?"

"Perfect."

Cami and Sage stayed and chatted for another hour before a glance at Sage told Cami it was time to say goodnight. "Thanks for a most entertaining evening, gentlemen." Vince's family had long-since returned home.

"You're welcome." Vince stood and helped Cami to her feet.

"It's time I left, too. I'll walk with you," Joel said, and came alongside Sage.

"Be back soon," Vince told his friends and the two couples walked off together.

Vince took Cami's hand again as they headed for her car. Joel and Sage followed behind.

"I'm glad you could both join us tonight," Vince said.

"Thanks for inviting us. Your family's nice and so are your friends. In fact, Jeremy's really great, I think maybe Sage's comment to him might be about me." Cami stopped teasing when Vince bumped her with his shoulder.

"Don't you start talking about my friends like that or I'll get a complex."

"I doubt it. You don't seem like the insecure type to me."

"Shows what you know. Most every guy is the insecure type when they're around beautiful, sophisticated, funny women." He sent her a flirtatious glance, then looked over his shoulder. "Now, for tomorrow. You sure you don't want to join us, Sage?"

"Quite sure." The response was emphatic.

"Do you need some extra help with your ground crew?" Joel asked, ever formal and distant. "Since Jeremy and Gage are busy. I'd like to see how it works."

"I can always use an extra set of hands," Vince agreed.

Joel turned to Sage. "You want to ride along with me? We can join them here for the main parade. I wouldn't want you to be all alone."

She hesitated for only a moment. "Sure. I'll come to the launch site with Cami and you can meet us there."

"Great! My family would love to have you all join us for whatever part of the day you'd like." Vince slid his fingers through Cami's and gave them a quick squeeze. "We'll have to leave at the crack of dawn to get set up and in the air on time. I'm more than happy to pick you up."

"How early?" She only winced a little when she realized she'd have to wake up before five. "I'm up for it. Stop by for us on your way out there."

"Will do." He stopped when they reached the car and let Joel and Sage walk past them. "I'll see you bright and early."

Cami unlocked the car remotely for Sage, then shifted to face Vince. "I'll be ready."

"Good." He lifted a hand, ran his finger along the right side of her jaw. His eyes said he wanted to kiss her, and he held her gaze for a long moment before putting a few more inches between them. "See you soon."

"Yeah, bright and early." Shivers rose on Cami's neck and shoulder where he'd touched her. With some effort, she pulled away and took the two steps to her door. She was both glad he hadn't followed through with the kiss, and a little disappointed. "Good night."

As they pulled out of the parking lot, Cami enjoyed the hum of excitement zipping through her veins when she thought of the next day's balloon ride, and considered her relationship with Vince could make her summer blues stay far, far away.

When they made it through the center of town at a crawl so as not to hit pedestrians, Cami noticed Joel behind them in his Jeep. She looked at Sage, who was staring out the window. A pang of guilt flashed through her. "Look, I'm sorry about what I said. I didn't mean for it to sound like that."

"Yes you did. But don't worry, I'm used to it. And I shouldn't have said anything to Jeremy, it just popped out. Next time I'll keep it to myself." Her tone was light and unconcerned, but she didn't look back at Cami.

"I'm not trying to hurt your feelings."

"Just leave it, Cami. I'll try not to embarrass you again. But don't be surprised when I'm right. I tend to be."

Cami glanced in her rearview mirror as she pulled in front of her house and noticed Joel parking at the much-smaller place next door. "Joel is our neighbor." She needed a change of subject.

"Yeah. He mentioned that." Sage straightened, grabbing her things.

When they parked in the garage, Sage hurried from the car, not saying anything as they separated to their rooms for the night.

Cami thought she ought to be happy that Sage would avoid her now, but she felt bad about embarrassing her in front of near strangers. She decided to worry about it later. She had notes to make from her chat with Gage earlier.

CHAPTER 12

Cami couldn't help but grin as she answered the door early the next morning. Vince stood on the other side, and the sky was starting to turn navy with the coming dawn. "Good morning."

"Hey. Are you ladies ready to go?" He brushed the hair back from his face and took a quick scan over her blue jean shorts and form-fitting spring-green blouse. "You might want a jacket; it can get pretty cool if we get as much altitude as I expect."

"I'm prepared." She gestured behind her to the jacket lying across a nearby chair. "Sage should be here any second." She'd been down for breakfast earlier.

As if in answer, the sound of steps on the balcony echoed down to them, and Sage descended the stairs wearing a red, white, and blue T-shirt and slim khaki shorts. Her dark curls were caught back in a white baseball cap. "Let me grab my bag," she said and moved to the kitchen.

"I wasn't sure if you ladies would actually be ready. My sisters have a habit of keeping me waiting for fifteen or twenty minutes whenever I'm supposed to meet them somewhere or pick them up."

Cami smiled, liking the way fondness entered his voice

when he talked about his family. "Dad didn't tolerate tardiness well." George hadn't been a bear about it, but it irked him, and she'd never wanted to displease him.

"No, he didn't." Vince tugged at an errant curl by her face and tucked it behind her ear. "You miss him."

She wanted to deny it, but she couldn't. "Yeah. I'm not too thrilled with him right now, but I miss him."

Sage reappeared, wearing a sweater and with a backpack hooked over one shoulder. "Let's go."

"Going hiking?" Vince asked while Cami grabbed her jacket. He checked out the hemp sandals on Sage's feet, which were definitely not hiking appropriate.

"No, just my camera, some extra bottled water, and something to collect flowers in case I find a few blooms I want to press. You said we might launch from a meadow, right?"

"Yeah. It's not peak time for flowers, but I'm sure you'll find a few that interest you." He held the door open so the ladies could precede him, waiting while Sage set the alarm, and double-checked the door lock after he'd pulled it closed.

They rounded the edge of the garage and Cami could see the basket and a huge canvas bag sticking up above the sides of Vince's truck bed. Excitement shot through her. "How far away is it?"

"Not too far, maybe ten minutes." Vince pulled the passenger door open for them and assisted Cami and Sage inside before circling around to the driver's door.

Cami tried not to squeeze too close to Vince in the cab, but it wasn't built for three adults. She found herself straddling the stick shift, hip to hip with Vince as he pulled onto the road. His cologne wafted her direction, an intoxicating mix of spice, musk and man. "Do you usually launch from the same place?"

"It depends on the wind currents. I actually got permission from a few property owners for launching, and before I came to get you, I checked the wind patterns to see which location would work best for the area where I want to set down. Now we'll have to see if I actually get to land where I want. You can't guide a balloon to land where you want it to; it follows the air flow around it, so you have to know wind patterns before you launch."

"Really? I didn't feel much of a breeze when we got into the truck, so is it possible we'll go up, and right back down in the same place again?"

"No." Vince chuckled as he changed gears, resting his wrist on her knee, but keeping his hand on the gear shift. "It may seem like there's no real breeze here, but if you get up a little higher, the currents change and there will be wind. And though I checked the wind patterns, the guys on the ground will still have to follow us because I never know for sure where I'll end up."

"That's why it's called a chase car," Sage piped up.

"Right." Vince took them around another corner and shifted down. Once they were going at a normal speed, he moved his hand back to Cami's knee, setting it there lightly, heating her bare skin.

"Gage and Jeremy talked like they usually crew for you," Sage said.

"Yeah, we're all commercial certified hot air balloon pilots and take turns going up. We have a few local kids who like to crew with us. Two of them are working on getting certified as well."

"Do you have to take formal lessons?" Cami asked, trying to focus on his words, and not on the hand on her knee.

Vince turned onto a dirt road. "Not like when you want to pilot a plane. There's a written test, then you have to work with a licensed instructor, and log a certain number of hours and stuff. It depends on what level of certificate you want. Kids can get a commercial certificate when they're only eighteen."

"How incredible. So how old do you have to be to become an instructor?" Eighteen seemed insanely young to Cami, but if they could drive a car at sixteen, why not, she decided. People were far less likely to crash in mid-air than on the twisty mountain roads.

It was getting light already and Cami spotted Joel standing between a red SUV and his Jeep in a meadow.

There wasn't much time for questions as Vince greeted everyone and made introductions. The guys pulled the equipment out of the truck bed, and Sage said she was going to scout out some flowers.

"Don't you want to watch the balloon get set up?" Cami asked.

"I've done it before, and it'll be a few minutes before it starts to rise. I'll be back soon." She turned and headed toward a patch of color a hundred yards off.

"Hey, where are you going?" Joel called out to Sage.

"Don't worry, I'll stay in sight. Just checking out some flowers," she called back over her shoulder.

Cami noticed Joel didn't seem to like Sage wandering away, and kept glancing back at her, scanning the surroundings every few minutes. What was with him? Once a SEAL, always a SEAL, she decided.

Turning back to the setup, Cami watched as they unfurled the balloon fabric from the huge canvas bag and pulled it out along the ground. She helped unfold it, so it lay more or less flat while Vince removed a huge fan from the truck bed and set it up.

"I guess it takes a lot of air to fill one of those things," Cami said when she came back over to him, wishing she'd worn long pants. She burrowed deeper into her jacket for warmth.

"*Those things* are called envelopes," Vince said with a grin. "And yeah, they take a while to fill. You want to take a corner of the envelope and hold it open for me?" When she lifted it so the air would blow into the fabric, a freckled teen named Cory grabbed the other side of the hole and helped hold it open. Vince yanked on a string and started the gas-fed fan.

The air rushed at Cami, and her hair whipped around her face and tangled behind her. The fabric jerked in her hands, rippling as the envelope slowly filled with air.

Vince set the fan to the correct angle, then turned back to the basket behind him. He and Joel lifted the burner into place on top of the basket and fastened it, before leaning it onto its side, so the burner would face the balloon. They shifted it closer, then Vince returned to the fan to check the angle.

It did take a while to get sufficient air into the envelope, but it wasn't as bad as Cami had expected. Even so, she was freezing by the time Vince directed the first burst of flames into the envelope.

Once he started heating the air, it didn't take long for the balloon to become upright. The crew surrounded the basket, holding on to keep it on the ground as Vince helped Cami inside.

Sage wandered back, her bag slung over one shoulder again. "It's a beautiful balloon, and a great day for a ride."

"I couldn't agree more," Vince said as he vaulted into the basket. He checked the business radio in the instrument panel to make sure he could speak to the ground crew. "We're good to go. Catch you all when we land again."

CHAPTER 13

The guys hopped off the edge of the basket and it started to rise, bobbing up above the ground and gaining altitude quickly. "What if the radio hadn't worked?" she asked.

"We have walkie-talkies for backup, they're good up to two-thousand feet, but the radio is better."

Cami waved to Sage and the others as the distance between them quickly lengthened. She peered up into the bright jewel tones of the envelope above them as the sun broke over the top of the mountain and radiated light down on them. "It's gorgeous. How long have you had the balloon?"

"A couple of years. We might make it through next summer with this envelope, if we're lucky, then we'll either have her overhauled or replaced. They rarely make it more than five-hundred hours. It's better here than some places because we're cooler, but eventually the heat from the burner takes its toll."

"And what about the rest of this stuff?" She gestured to the basket and instrument panel. "What's all this equipment for if you can't steer the balloon?"

"I can steer it, if I want to go in the direction the wind allows." He pointed out the altimeter, compass, and fuel gauge for the burner, and showed her how to work the business radio so he could chat with the chase crew.

The fresh morning air called to Cami as she soaked in the beauty of the valley. She was fascinated as Vince pointed out the local sights, and found she was more impressed than ever when she saw the DiCarlo resort from the air—it was spectacular. "We should get a shot of the resort from up here for the website." She leaned forward on the basket and stared out at the world below them.

"Good idea. I bet Jeremy would be happy to take one next time he comes up." He stared at the grounds. "So, has anyone told you about your resident ghost yet?"

"We already have a ghost?" Cami was amused. "I thought someone was supposed to die there before you could have ghosts on the property."

"Yeah, well, the property existed before the DiCarlo empire bought it, didn't it?"

She nodded her acknowledgement. "So tell me about the ghost. Has it been around for long?"

Vince smiled and leaned toward her, his voice lowering theatrically. "There's a legend of a Mexican family mining in the valley who struck it rich. When local vandals learned about the find, they went to the house—which was supposed to be situated right where the hotel is now—killing the wife and children while the husband was away, and stealing all of the gold before torching the place. The husband returned home to find his home in ashes and the charred remains of his family inside, a tomahawk sticking out of his wife's head. He reportedly spent the rest of his life and then his death, haunting the property, a broken man."

Cami hoped the story wasn't all that well known—just the thought made her shiver. "That's a little creepy. So have there been reports of sightings over the years?"

"Plenty of them. And they've increased since your father broke ground on the hotel. One of the local crackpots claims the construction has disturbed the dead."

"I wonder if it will hurt or improve our room bookings if the story gets out to guests." Was there a way to use it to their advantage, since it was lingering around anyway? She dismissed the idea—it didn't exactly work well with the company reputation and would definitely cause issues with the normal clientele.

"Not too worried, then?" Vince asked.

"I'm taking a positive attitude. I doubt it will make headlines in hotel news unless we make a big deal over it. Our guests rarely care much about local legends." And if anything popped up, she'd bury it.

"Glad to hear it." Vince reached out and slid a curl behind her ear.

Cami touched her mussed curls and tried to make order of them with her fingers. "Now I know why Sage wanted her space while the fan was on," she joked. "I've got to be a mess."

Vince just smiled. "You look fine, happy."

"How could I be otherwise?" she said as she met his eyes and felt a shiver of attraction shoot through her. She wondered if this was more than a passing flirtation and decided to test it. "I have a confession to make."

"A confession? Sounds heavy. Don't tell me you like Greek food." His face was so serious, it threw her for a second.

She felt the corner of her mouth twitch at the way he'd responded. He always kept her guessing, doing the unexpected. Cami found him intriguing and more than a little alluring. "Yes, I do, but I didn't know it was a sin requiring confession. I'll keep it in mind."

He took her hand in his. "I'll appreciate it, and forgive you for your unhealthy addiction to Gyros, if that's the problem."

She leaned in and lowered her voice slightly. "It's worse—Moussaka."

He tipped his head away as if it was a blow to his sensibilities. "Don't tell me. I might not get over it." He smiled and rubbed his thumb across her palm. "So what dastardly thing have you done requiring confession?"

She studied him, intrigued by all the sides making up the man, and knew she'd barely scratched the surface. "You may have gathered, I'm not entirely thrilled with the things I've learned about my father in the past couple of months."

"Couldn't blame you. It's an awful lot to deal with."

She blew out a breath. "Okay, so I'm going to try not to stumble around on this too much. Normally I wouldn't admit this, but at the moment I'm pretty big on straight-up honesty." She hoped she didn't offend him—that the way she ended the confession would make it more palatable.

"Honesty's always a good thing." He'd moved closer. *Had* he moved closer? She wasn't sure. He must have inched in.

"My father has always pushed me on guys who had flash and power and were upwardly mobile. He favored post-graduate degrees and suave exteriors. Maybe because that's what he was—all suave exterior." She tasted the bitterness in her mouth and swallowed it back. "Sorry. I don't know if I'll ever be able to forgive him for his serial affairs, even if I become as tight with the other daughters as he wanted." She doubted that would ever happen.

"I understand." Vince's voice softened. "It's a big thing to handle all at once, and the vow to love, honor, and cherish doesn't have an amnesty clause if you suddenly decide you want a piece on the side."

"Right." His words soothed her. "So I meet you, a little unkempt, two-day beard growth, down digging in the dirt, and though I could tell from the first that you were a great guy, you're so unlike anyone I'd ever considered dating before. When I came out onto the patio the other day, it was with more than half the thought that you were the type my father *wouldn't* want me to spend time with."

He leaned back. "Really?" His expression showed amusement rather than offense. "What was the rest of it?"

She pursed her lips. If she was going to be honest, she might as well go for broke. "You're handsome, appealing in a rough-edged way. Polite, great with your niece, and hard working. All good qualities."

He nodded, but kept his thoughts to himself—if you didn't count the almost predatory grin sneaking onto his lips.

She rushed to finish, "And then I spent the day with you, and discovered you're well informed, funny, bright, great with people. The rough edges only make you more appealing. So if you're not offended by my comments, I find I wouldn't mind getting to know you better, and it has nothing to do with what my father would think." Or Trent, but she wasn't about to get *that* honest. Not today, anyway.

Vince took a lock of her auburn curls and twisted it between his fingers. "Well, as long as we're doing confessions, I have one as well."

The intent expression in his eyes made her nervous and she tried to soften the mood. "Oh? Do you have a strange fascination with belly dancers?"

His quick grin flared. "Yes, but most straight guys do, so

it's hardly strange or worthy of confession. Actually, I was going to say I spent a lot of time one-on-one with your father when we were developing the landscaping plan for both the house and the hotel."

"Not surprising, considering how much he loved gardening. He planned the yard at his home as well." She remembered him showing her the latest layouts every few weeks as he refined them, followed by regular updates on the improvements once work began.

"He mentioned it, and he talked about you a lot. All of his girls, actually, but especially you." His voice went low and a bit husky and his gaze captured hers, making it impossible to look away.

"Really?" The thought her father had spoken of her so much pricked the cold shell she'd been trying to keep wrapped over her heart, and she didn't want that. She forced herself not to move away from Vince despite the emotional step back she took after his announcement.

He ran his fingers down her arm to her elbow, and back up to the edge of her capped sleeves. "Yes, in fact, he went on and on about how much alike we were in our dedication to serving our clients, and willingness to think outside the box. He talked about your abilities with PR, and in charming even the most difficult guest. He made quite a case for you, enough to remove all doubt he'd like to see us together."

Completely the opposite of what she'd thought, and how did she feel about that? Manipulated again? There wasn't time to process her emotions. "Really? So you just fell in line? And so did I." She muttered the last as she finally put some space between them. Worse than she'd imagined. Her father was behind Vince's interest in her. George couldn't stop himself from meddling, but this wasn't at all like the other times he'd suggested she *befriend* someone.

It was a small basket, though, and there wasn't much room to move around, so even with the shift away from Vince, they were still close. He slid nearer, blocking her into the corner, a hand on the edge to keep his balance, eyes solidly on her. He went on as if she hadn't interrupted. "I admit, my first thought was you must be very plain if he had to make your case. Either that or you weren't very good at personal relationships."

Cami made a humming noise indicating she was listening. She wasn't sure how else to respond. His nearness made her chest tight and the scent of his cologne had her pulse racing.

"I Googled you, found a photo from a news item. My thought was, man, the woman has a face on her." He slid a finger down her cheek.

She felt a light warmth of pleasure in her chest at his words, but fought to appear unaffected. "Funny, I've never met anyone who wasn't born with a face. Most everyone is issued one en utero."

He refused to be distracted. "So I thought, hey, maybe she just shows well in pictures. Jeremy has some serious skills with a computer, so I know what can be done with a little time. But then I met you, and you wore those great heels that made your legs look about a mile long, and this sweet smile though I could sense you weren't really happy to be there. And the face was even better in person than it was in photos."

He inched closer, ran his fingers under her chin so it tipped up to him. "I thought it must be a faulty personality, because the outside package sure is amazing. But last night you played with my dogs and were sweet with my niece and parents, you chatted and laughed with my friends and ate that diet-killer deep fried candy bar. I realized your dad wasn't trying to foist you off on anyone. I have the funny feeling we might make a nice fit." He shifted closer, and his mouth hovered a breath away from hers until her lips tingled and ached for contact. "So I hope you aren't going to step back, just to defy your father."

"There's nowhere else to go." She meant it literally, as her back was to the wall of the basket, but that wasn't all. Deciding she didn't care if Vince dug holes in the ground and barely scraped by, she leaned in and brushed her lips across his.

He tipped his head to the side and pulled her closer, taking the kiss deeper. One hand speared into her hair, while the other cradled her cheek, a gentle taste, a growing quest to learn more. She slid her hands around his waist and clung.

Vince lightened the kiss and stepped back. He glanced at the instrument panel and hit the burner again and it filled the air with a roar for several seconds. "I better not forget where we are. We need the altitude if we're going to find a good place to land." His words sounded calm and unaffected, if you ignored the husky note to his voice.

Cami sucked in a breath, trying to settle her whirling mind. His kiss was unexpectedly more than she'd experienced before in a first kiss. Friends, books and television said first kisses could be like that, but this was the first time she'd ever felt her knees go soft. She let her mind settle while he added altitude to the balloon so it would catch a different wind current.

"How are you doing?" he asked after a moment, his smile growing.

85

In for a penny. "If you were trying to find a way to convince me I don't want to spite myself just to show my father he was wrong, you found it."

He grinned at her "It wasn't my intent, but I'm hardly going to argue with results."

CHAPTER 14

They touched down on an empty baseball diamond twenty minutes later after a return to neutral topics. The basket bumped against the ground, jarring Cami's knees, though she'd bent them slightly to cushion the blow as Vince had directed. Joel, Jeremy, and the teens rushed to help them secure the basket and begin pulling the balloon down. Cami climbed out of the basket, laughing as she approached Sage. The kiss hadn't been the only thrilling part of the ride, and she hoped she got another chance to go up. "That was awesome. I hope you weren't too bored."

"Joel entertained me. You're glowing—it must have been a nice ride." Sage's eyes sparkled at Cami. "What did I say about meeting your match?"

"I don't know about that, but the side trip should be fun." Cami straightened her ruffled hair. They almost overshot their destination when the breeze had grown stronger than expected. "It was wonderful. I definitely want to try it again someday."

"Good. Hey, you were probably too busy to pay attention to your cell phone up there, but Lana reached me a while ago and said we'd want to check out a news story. She sent you a link." She pulled out her phone, flashed it. "Mine doesn't have the Internet. Maybe you'll have better luck."

Cami pulled out her Droid and checked the screen, finding a message from Lana. Strange she hadn't heard it, but she'd been a bit distracted for most of the trip. The cell signal had probably been stronger in the balloon than it was now as she barely had one bar. She pocketed the phone again.

"I'll have to wait until we get back into town. The signal there's better." She eyed Sage, realizing the strain between them had lessened and hoped they could get back to being, well, not friends, but not angry with each other, either. "Why don't you have a smart phone? You've got scads of things to keep track of, and it's only going to get worse. We'll talk to Lana, have her get you one. We can set it up to sync with your terminal at the hotel."

Sage shook her head. "No way. Those things confuse me."

"You'll catch on soon, and then you'll wonder what you ever did without it." Seeing the balloon back on the ground, she tugged Sage's arm and they hurried to help pack it.

The parade was about to start when they all jogged up to the spot in the crowd Vince's family had staked out. Cami greeted everyone, and kept her ears open for names, to try to pick up the ones she'd confused or forgotten since the previous evening. The event opened with the military bringing the flags, followed by the golf course's float.

Cami leaned over to Sage. "We need to think about doing a float for next year. Maybe something highlighting your spa? Think about it; we'll talk to Lana." They would be employing a lot of locals and wanted to find a way to let residents feel the resort was part of the community.

"Speaking of, did you check out the link she sent you?"

"Oh, right." Cami dug out her phone again and clicked the link, she called out praise for the high school band as they marched past in perfect rhythm. Gage made a comment which made his two friends laugh out loud. Cami smiled at them ribbing each other, then glanced back at the screen.

Her smile died as the news article popped up on the Chicago area gossip magazine.

DiCarlo heiresses squander time and money at summer retreat

Hotel magnate George DiCarlo has been in the ground only six weeks and already his daughters are sitting back enjoying their freedom. Many people have questioned their ability to put together the quality of hotel that has long given DiCarlo his good name. Concerns seem to be justified, as the daughters don't appear to be working hard to get things ready for opening day in less than two months.

While vacationing in the Rocky Mountain town of Juniper Ridge this week, eldest daughter, Camellia DiCarlo, and second eldest, Sage Parker mixed with locals, enjoyed fair food, and got it going on with a few of the down-home country boys.

A picture of Cami and Vince standing beside her Z4 the previous evening, close enough they could have been kissing popped up next. The caption read, "*Lawn mower extraordinaire seems to have caught Camellia's fancy—and her lips—during a heated embrace in public before they took things to a more private venue.*"

Directly below it was a shot of Sage sitting between Gage and Jeremy, laughing with them, her eyes lit up. "*Sage seems unable to choose one of the handsome hunks—ski bum or photography buff.*"

The article went on to question whether any of the sisters was taking their responsibilities seriously and what it portended for the business's chance of success.

Cami was speechless, unable to decide whether she was more shocked, horrified, furious, or amused by the mix of ridiculous supposition and outright lies.

"What is it? You look ready to punch someone." Sage reached for the phone.

Cami scrolled the article back to the top and handed the phone over, trying to keep her reaction under control. Sage wouldn't be used to the horrible things the media came up with. "Don't take it too seriously. Gossip rags are always searching for an angle." The idea of the article winding up all over the country at grocery store stands made Cami's stomach tighten in a knot, however. She'd have to call Lana as soon as she could pull away for a minute.

There was a noise almost like a whimper, and Cami saw Sage with her hand over her mouth. Her face had lost all color. "It says where we are," she whispered. "I knew something was going to happen, I just didn't know what."

"And no publicity is bad publicity," Cami said, though as they weren't rock stars, it wasn't true. She wasn't buying into Sage's prescience. She eased the phone from Sage's white-knuckled grip. She wasn't as sanguine as the comment made her sound—not nearly—but Cami was at least used to living in

90

a fish bowl, and Sage was not. "Everyone pretty well knew where we are anyway. Most of the terms of the will were spelled out pretty clear, and we've been touting this new hotel everywhere." Still, she found herself checking for cameras pointed their direction, and eyeing Jeremy with suspicion as he picked out a shot of the cheerleaders dancing by.

"Hey, what's wrong?" Vince asked as he leaned in to Cami from the other side.

She pasted on a smile and hoped she could ease the concern in his eyes. This was not the time. "Nothing much, minor hotel stuff. Nothing that can't wait until after the parade, at least. Tell me about the horseback riding club. Do you know of anyone in the area who takes paying customers out for trail rides?"

He didn't appear convinced that there was nothing to worry about, but he allowed the change of subject. Cami squeezed Sage's elbow comfortingly when the worry continued to crease the woman's brow, then buried her own concerns until she had time to think it over later.

When the parade ended and they had made the rounds of the park again, Joel dropped the girls off at home to pick up Sage's car and the cake Mrs. Grady had made for them the previous day and followed them to Vince's parents' home. Cami rode with Sage while Vince swung by his place to grab the two elephant hybrids he said were dogs. Cami took the opportunity to call Lana and chat.

"It's about time you called. It's been hours since I sent you the link. I called four times in the past hour," Lana said in lieu of hello.

"Sorry, I couldn't hear it over the parade. Vince has been introducing me to lots of the local business owners. It's been very productive."

"Yeah, yeah, can we get back to the issue at hand?"

"Stop freaking out. Yes, I'm going to do my best to track down where the pictures and article came from, but it's bound to create more speculation and interest in the hotel. I wouldn't worry about it. I popped onto Twitter and left a note about enjoying the local color during the holiday. No one's going to think twice about it." If they were lucky, she thought.

"Yeah, you weren't here for the Whitneys' annual party, though, were you?"

"When was that?"

"Yesterday." Lana huffed." I can't believe you're there taking it easy and I'm dealing with the Whitneys and Carters. Seriously, this gets worse every year. Anyway, I overheard a rather well-projected whisper about Dad wanting to keep us all under the same roof so he could have someone babysit us. There was the expected comment about Blake being moved to the location as babysitter, and how Alex is supposed to be all but moving in as well—I had to ask Alex for confirmation. He denied it, though."

The role of listening ear wasn't new to Cami, so she said what Lana needed to hear. "You know Dad had total trust in you—he wouldn't risk the business if he didn't. You're going to do a smashing job. We all are, and soon everyone else will know it. Settle down."

"I don't like it, Cami. Something feels off."

"So noted. Now, go enjoy your holiday, put this aside. When you get back here next week we'll review the damage, and anything else you've been able to glean on the gossip mart. Then we can handle any problems. But there won't be anything major, so take it easy."

"It certainly looks like you're taking it easy." Lana paused. "Sorry I'm such a worrywart. What's up with you and Vince?

Were you actually kissing him, or was that a photography trick?"

"No kisses." She waited a beat. "*Last night*, anyway." She couldn't help but feel smug. Kissing was definitely one of his talents, and she had the feeling she hadn't seen anything yet. She had every intention of learning more about his skill in that area before this was over.

"All right, that's it! We're so having a long chat when I get back. Ugg, here comes Clarissa Clearwater. Gotta go."

"Bye." Cami chuckled as she hit the *end* button. "Better you than me, sis." Clarissa Clearwater would be sure to share every tidbit of gossip with Lana, but she would expect the same back in return. It would be a miserable tight wire for Lana to maneuver. Yet another reason Cami was grateful to be in Colorado for the next year.

"You aren't worried, are you?" Sage asked.

Cami shrugged as they pulled in beside Gage's truck. Sage and Lana were worried for all of them, though it didn't stop her from seething over the article. If she could smooth the crease in Sage's brow, acting as if she weren't disturbed would be worth it. "No point in getting upset before we see where things are going. We were bound to get a few nasty jabs. This will all sort itself out in a while." She would make sure of it.

CHAPTER 15

"So what's been bothering you?" Vince asked as he walked Cami to the front door after the fireworks ended. It had been a wonderful day full of laughter, happy chatter and sufficient food to feed a crowd twice the size of the forty-plus that had gathered in the Talmadge's yard. And the local fireworks had been spectacular.

"What?" Cami smiled, trying to make him think it was his imagination.

"Sorry, you can't fool me. Something's been on your mind since the parade. What were you and Sage reading on your phone?"

Cami debated for a moment before pulling up the article again. She handed it over to him. His brows lifted as he read, but he didn't seem surprised or upset. "Interesting. It makes me sound like a glorified ditch digger. Not that there's anything wrong with ditch digging in general, of course, and my employee list may be like a gnat versus a whale compared to what you'll be hiring shortly, but it's a living." He chuckled. "And the bit about Gage being a ski bum—priceless! I can't wait to show it to him." He handed the phone back. "Is this article going to cause problems?"

Cami shrugged, not wanting him to know it disturbed her, even if it didn't qualify as a serious crisis. "PR wise, it's nothing much on its own. I'll check it out, but I'm not going to lose a lot of sleep." She slid the phone into her pocket. "It makes me wonder who was taking the pictures, though. Jeremy's in one of them, so unless he had some help—"

His voice was hard when he cut her off. "Don't go there. None of my family—and that includes Jeremy and Gage, who might as well be my brothers—would write something like this or try to make a quick buck at your expense. Earn money from business arrangements with you, sure. If you want professional photos of events or of your new facilities, Jeremy will be happy to help you out for a fee. And if you want to set up the deal for the skiers you were speaking with Gage about, he'll certainly be on board, but no one's going to hose you like this."

Cami studied his face but saw nothing to hint he wasn't being sincere. "Thanks. I appreciate your candor. And I believe both of those options have possibilities. Jeremy's name was on the list of locals Dad mentioned we should consider making arrangements with. I'll bring it up with Lana and Delphi." She saw the defensiveness melt from his stance and decided to explain further. "Okay, I don't know anyone here, so I don't know who or what was out of place yesterday. With everyone in town for the holidays, even you probably don't know. In fact, it could have been someone who happened across us and thought they could make a quick buck. Like I said, it's not a big deal, it just made me wonder."

"Well, so long as we're clear." Vince tucked some hair back behind her ear, brushing his fingers across her sensitive neck. "I didn't mean to open a can of worms right now. I had a great time with you today." He leaned in and rubbed his mouth across hers, lingering there until she slid into his arms, shifting her head to take a little more. She loved kissing this man.

"I wondered what your week looks like," he said when he pulled back. "I told Gage I'd give him a hand with the mountain bike festival after I finish my daily rounds. I should be free by Wednesday night, though, if you'd like to grab a bite?"

She smiled. "I think I would. You know how to reach me."

"And maybe we could take your car for a drive. I could make sure the engine is running right." His eyes glimmered with hope.

Cami pulled away, turning to the car where Sage waited for her. "Only if I'm driving, Vince."

"Someday."

She laughed as she wriggled her fingers at him over her shoulder.

Vince smiled as the customer exited his office door and turned back to his paperwork, fighting the scowl that wanted to slide onto his face. The day had been insane, and the evenings were worse as he and Jeremy helped Gage with the mountain bike revelers. The festival ended the next afternoon, though, and Vince would be free to spend the evening with the lovely Camellia.

The thought of lingering over a quiet meal with her brightened his mood. Though he ought to focus all of his attention on work—summer was his busiest time and business was booming—Vince was fascinated by Camellia. The fact that

96

her father had all but arranged their marriage should have turned Vince off, as it had his friends to two of George's other daughters. But now he'd gotten to know Cami a little, he wasn't going anywhere.

He considered most of the local eating establishments and rejected them in turn until he thought of a charming Italian place. Great atmosphere, quiet, with slightly more privacy than the average restaurant. It would suit his needs perfectly.

He smiled as he picked up the ringing phone. "Nature's Garden. This is Vince, how can I help you?"

"Hey, it's Cory. I'm here with Mrs. Stuart and she wants you to swing by and talk to her about adding a pond in her backyard."

Vince loved doing water features. They were his specialty, though he didn't get to install them as often as he'd like. "Great," he flipped through his calendar. "How does tomorrow afternoon work for her? I can manage a consult about two."

Cory conferred with the client and passed on the woman's agreement.

Vince checked to see what else was on Cory's schedule for the day. "Thanks, and Cory, don't forget to check the Sullivans' azaleas. She said they were wilting."

"I'm headed there now." Cory said goodbye and hung up.

The kid was good at his job and reliable. In another year or so Vince might let him help with the design work. Visualizing the shape and flow of the Stuart's yard, Vince imagined a couple of possibilities.

It didn't take long for his mind to meander back to Cami. He smiled and returned to work.

CHAPTER 16

Cami continued to make contacts with local businesses, collecting brochures for companies who rented out and guided groups on ATVs, mountain bikes and horseback riding. She discussed package agreements for the ski resort with Gage, and met with local golf courses within an hour's drive.

Job applications were rolling in. Cami talked with the new HR manager, who happened to be Sage's half-brother, Harrison. He would be joining them on the mountain before the end of the week. If there was one thing Cami could say about her dad, he liked to keep it all in the family, more or less. She wasn't sure if that was an advantage or not.

Lana arrived back at the house Wednesday night, an hour before Vince was due to pick up Cami for their date. Soon after her arrival, she came knocking on Cami's open door.

"So what's the 411 on you and Vince? A second date already?" Lana asked as she breezed into the room and perched on the corner of the bed.

Cami sat at her mirror and tweaked her hair. "It's just a second date." But she could see the smug gleam in her reflection, and a glance at Lana confirmed she saw it as well.

Vince had called to verify the time he'd pick her up, but they'd both been on the run, and the conversation had only lasted a couple of minutes. She couldn't wait to have more time with him.

"Spill. When did he kiss you the first time?" Lana demanded. "I can't believe you refused to give me any details!"

They could have been back in high school, Cami thought, but she had missed the close camaraderie the two of them had lost as their lives headed in different directions and different cities over the past decade. "He took me for a hot air balloon ride on the Fourth. It was charming and exciting, and almost nauseating because we climbed over three-thousand feet."

Lana put a hand to her stomach. "Holy smokes, that's high. Is there actually oxygen up there? I mean, we're nearly twelve-thousand feet already. It's a wonder we didn't all get altitude sickness when we came here last time."

"Don't be dramatic. Anyway, the flight was amazing, and he was great . . . and fun, suave and smart. The man has so many angles I hardly know what new facet I'll uncover next." She glided her lipstick on, rubbed her lips together, then checked it out in the mirror. "Anyway, I decided to be honest and tell him I first flirted with him because I figured Dad would never approve."

Lana's eyes grew round and her mouth fell open for a second. "I can't believe you said that! Cami, I've never known you to be straight-up rude to a nice guy before."

"Not nice ones, no. But then I told him he was way more than I thought, and I was having fun with him." She frowned slightly as she picked through her cosmetics to find the right blush. "He told me Dad tried to convince him the two of us would be perfect together, and Vince had decided I must either be ugly or socially inept, until he met me." She grinned at her sister in the mirror. "It was quite enlightening, and honestly, only intrigued me more—which doesn't make any sense, but there you go."

Lana's eyes bugged out. "So when did he kiss you? Before or after your heart-to-heart?"

"After. Smack dab after, and I have to say, Trent so pales in comparison in the kissing department. Trent could probably have taken lessons from the teenaged Vince and learned something, the man is seriously talented." It felt good to say it, especially with the nasty aftertaste her ex had left after his last visit.

Lana sat in surprise for a long moment. "Okay, that's . . . hmmm. Isn't it great when the guy really knows what he's doing? Night and day difference. I remember . . . Well, anyway."

Cami twisted around in her chair and eyed her sister. "Whoa, who have you been kissing lately? I haven't heard about you with anyone for a while now. Almost a year. And why not?" She wiggled her eyebrows when she thought of Gage. "You know Vince has a couple of hot friends—"

This time it was Lana's turn to protest. She slashed her hand down, cutting off the comment. "No, we're not going there. No blind dates, no set ups, no men of any kind. Period."

Odd coming from a woman who had been pretty active on the dating scene since her teens, and Cami thought she sensed an edge of hurt in her sister's words. "You want to talk about it?"

Lana's face hardened. "No. Just go ahead and give me the lowdown on the contacts you've made this week."

Deciding it was okay to let Lana have her change of

subject—there wasn't time to needle an answer out of her right now anyway—Cami recapped her activities. "You'll find the contracts on your bedroom desk and I'll send you an email with my notes tonight so you can check them over in the morning." She slid her feet into a pair of silver, strappy, heeled sandals and checked her cute purple Dior dress in the full-length mirror. She looked good.

The doorbell rang and Cami grabbed her coordinating clutch and headed out.

Sage called up the stairs, "Cami, Vince is here."

Cami had to remind herself her sandals weren't made for rushing down stairs as she reached the open staircase leading to the great room. It was ridiculous how excited she was for this date—she wasn't a fresh-faced teen anxious to get to the prom.

Vince came into view, eyeing her as she descended. "Wow. Do you need more words, because I'm afraid if I try I'll trip over my own tongue," he said as she reached the bottom. He took her hands and pressed a kiss to her cheek.

The comment made her grin. "I think wow will do. And right back at ya." Whatever Cami had expected, it hadn't been the navy suit with a stark white pinstripe. He'd said to dress up, but she'd never imagined 'up' for him included a suit coat. He looked every bit as appealing clean shaven as he had with a sexy scruff of beard. "I admit, I'm not sure what you have in mind tonight."

A smile curved his lips. "Good." He turned to Lana. "It's good to see you again. Hope you don't mind me taking off with your sister when you probably just got in."

"I'll catch her when she comes back. It sounds as though she's been working hard all week. And Vince, sometime I'd like to take a ride in your balloon." She lifted a hand as she added a caveat, "But without the kissing, since she'd break off all of my fingers."

Cami rolled her eyes, but he laughed. "As soon as I get a chance I'll arrange to take you both up for a ride."

"I'm going to hold you to it. Now have a good evening."

"I guess we have her approval," Cami said as she gave Vince's hand a light tug toward the door. "See ya," she said to Sage as they walked by. The two of them had shared bits of conversation over the previous few days, but they'd both been very much wrapped in their own pursuits. Sage seemed to have put her hurt over Cami's thoughtless comments in the park behind her, but Cami couldn't forget them.

It occurred to her maybe Sage had been a little lonely in the past few days. Despite the free time on their hands, she rarely went anywhere besides the hotel. Cami pushed that to the corner of her mind to consider some other time—when she didn't have tall, dark, and handsome taking her out.

They rounded the patio to the driveway and she grinned as a classic Mustang in metallic blue came into view. She sent him a sideways glance. "Borrow it from Jeremy?" She was relieved as she'd only ever seen his truck and her dress and his four-wheel drive weren't a great combination.

He put a hand over his heart. "You wound me. Jeremy did help me fix it up, but this baby's mine. It's nothing compared to your Z4, of course."

"Few things are." But she loved the lines and angles of the Mustang. "What year is it?"

"1967." He opened the door for her. "I bought it when I was fourteen, spent the next two years pouring all my summer earnings into getting it to run." He shut the door when she was seated and circled around to his side. "Best investment I ever made," he said when he was putting on his seatbelt.

"I bet you got a lot of chicks with this car," she suggested, though she had the feeling she already knew the answer. It wouldn't have been a classic back when he was in high school, but a hot Mustang was a hot Mustang at any age.

He grinned but declined to answer, making her like him better for not bragging or denying the truth.

As they pulled onto the road, she asked, "So where are we going, anyway?"

"You'll see."

It ended up being a little mom-and-pop shop off the beaten path with fabulous pasta and a soft, romantic atmosphere.

"I never would've expected to find this here," Cami said as Vince held her hand across the table. The staff was friendly and her spinach linguini in pesto and the slice of tiramisu she'd shared with Vince had been incredible. "If it wouldn't offend Rosemary, I'd put a bug in Lana's ear about trying to steal the chef. On the other hand, we have three restaurants, and a number of openings coming up, maybe I will anyway."

Vince laughed. "Since Carlotta owns the place, I doubt even you or Lana could convince her to jump ship."

"Oh, well, you can't have everything." But she made a mental note to add it to the restaurant list for the concierges.

"How is Rosemary in the kitchen, anyway?"

Cami took a sip of her water; she'd stopped at a single glass of wine. "I hear she's fabulous, but I haven't had a chance to sample anything she's cooked yet—except espresso, and she's a whiz at that. Best on the *planet!*"

"And you?" He lifted her hands, kissed the backs of her

fingers slowly, eyes focused on her face. "What are you good at?"

She felt a frisson of anticipation rush through her at the contact. "I'm a whiz at a lot of things, and I can make my own meals when I must, but cooking isn't my biggest talent. You?"

"I make a mean spaghetti."

She couldn't look away, felt sucked into his dark gaze. "Yeah? Anything else?"

He turned her hand over and traced the inside of her fingers and along her palm with kisses, demonstrating how good he was at seducing a woman's senses. "Coffee. Cold cereal. Peanut butter sandwiches—I make the best you ever tasted."

Air shuddered into her lungs at his touch and the fluttering in her chest that he was so good at producing had returned. She wondered how such a simple touch could affect her so much. "Maybe I'll give them a try sometime."

"I'll make sure of it." He lowered her hand, his expression regretful. "I suppose we ought to head back. I have to be up before sunrise."

"Already?" She could have sworn they'd only been there for an hour or so.

He chuckled. "We've been here over three hours. I think they're hoping to close soon."

She glanced around them and realized there was only one other customer in the building. "Well, then." She pulled her hand free and stood. A glance at her watch proved it was nearly ten. "This was a great idea."

He tossed a tip onto the table as he'd already paid their tab. "I'm glad you approve." He threaded his fingers through hers and led her to the door. "I thought something different was in order, to show you I'm more than a glorified mower of lawns."

"I had already figured that out," she reminded him.

"Yes, so you said." They walked through the front gardens to an arch covered in climbing roses, still in bloom and filling the night with their soft fragrance. Twinkle lights had been wound into the arch and along the bushes beside the path. He turned her into his arms. "You're an amazing woman."

"I'm glad you think so." It was all she got out before he covered her mouth with his. This kiss was as different from the first as night from day. Where the first kiss had been gentle, sliding into sensual, this one started strong, and only grew deeper. He slid his hands up her arms—which were covered in goosebumps—and to her neck, tipped her head, and took it deeper.

Cami felt like she was drowning and didn't care about coming up for air. She held on and pulled him closer, tasting his mouth, nipping at his bottom lip.

When she eased back, she thought if he was going to make a habit of sending her head whirling, she'd have to stop wearing high heels. She felt wobbly and held onto his arm for support while she got her bearings. "You have a way of knocking me for a loop."

"The feeling's mutual." He took her elbow, steadying her, and they continued to his car.

After a far less explosive, but every bit as mind-numbing kiss when they reached her front door, Cami floated into the house to find Rosemary and Jonquil in the great room with Lana and Sage.

Lana smirked at her. "I'm glad you had a good time."

"I didn't say that." But she couldn't wipe the smile from her face.

"Like the stars in your eyes aren't enough? How stupid do you think we are?" Rosemary asked. She pushed a long fall of blonde hair behind her shoulder. "I'm almost surprised you noticed we were in the room."

Cami beamed at them. Then her brain kicked in and she saw the worry on their faces. Rosemary and Jonquil shouldn't have been there. When had they arrived? Had something happened after she'd turned off her phone? Her smile fell and she crossed to them. "What's going on?"

A frown came over Lana's face. "We didn't want to ruin your date. You'd better sit down. There's another media issue we need to handle."

CHAPTER 17

Cami stared at the news article Lana had brought up on her laptop.

Life of crime: Did Daddy DiCarlo make a big mistake?

As if the pictures of debauchery from a few days ago weren't enough, stories are flooding in about the other sisters in the DiCarlo debacle. Reports that Jonquil Chestnut has a history of theft and criminal behavior have been confirmed. Rosemary Keogh was expelled from more than one school for refusing to follow the rules, and actually held internships under two different chefs in Europe—which begs the question, did Daddy have to pay someone off so she could finish her training—training she apparently couldn't get anyone in the U.S. to give her?

The world waits to see if the daughters of hotel magnate George DiCarlo can pull off the launch of his newest resort.

Cami gnashed her teeth. "All right, I already know this is a load of crap, so tell me what really happened. If we're going to twist it back our way, I need all the facts." She looked at Jonquil.

Jonquil spread her hands. "The best I can think of is that I stole a candy bar when I was nine. My mom found it, took me back to the store, and arranged with the store owner for me to go in every afternoon for a week to sweep the floors. I didn't even get to keep the candy bar."

"And your supposed criminal record?" Cami asked.

Jonquil's lips twisted and she avoided eye contact. "I had too many parking tickets—give a girl a break; do you have any idea how hard it is to find a parking spot in Philly? Anyway, I didn't get them paid in a timely manner, and I ended up with a warrant for my arrest. A friend of mine worked on the force, mentioned it to me and I went in the next day and took care of it. I wasn't ever booked."

"All right. I'm surprised there was still a note anywhere about the warrant." Cami rubbed her temples. "Those should be easy to prove, but I want you to call your friend and find out why the warrant is still popping up under your name, and get it cleared out. If they're finding it, the warrant may still show it's valid."

Jonquil covered her mouth. "I didn't think of that."

Already feeling a little better, Cami turned to Rosemary. "Okay, spill, you rule breaker. What happened? Were you actually kicked out of your schools?"

Rosemary smirked. "Okay, I can't help it; I was a bit of a rebel. Dad always said I should've grown up in the sixties."

Not amused, Cami pinned her with a hard glare.

"Fine. You need to lighten up! I wasn't actually kicked out. We had an administrator at the school who was giving a teacher problems. She was a great teacher, totally dedicated, and didn't even have to work. She had plenty of money." She lounged back on the sofa.

When Cami kept staring at her, Rosemary shrugged and continued on. "Anyway, I was on the student council when she tendered her resignation in the middle of the year because the dude was picking at her so much. We talked about it and decided to stage a walkout. I headed the whole thing. The administrator quit that day and left town, and the teacher stayed. If I served a week's after-school detention, it was well worth the price."

"And what else? I understand you actually completed two full internships in Europe with chefs who focused on different things. The second one was a pastry chef, right?" Cami leaned back in the chair, not quite ready to relax, but feeling a little better about things.

"Exactly. So it's total crap."

"And before that?"

Rosemary's lips pursed. "Okay, there was one more situation, but I was framed."

Framed? Really? Cami wanted to reach out and smack Rosemary for not getting to the point. She'd been in such a great mood ten minutes earlier. "Details. Now."

"Keep your shirt on, or should I say, your dress, and did I mention how much I love those sandals? Wow!" She shifted further into the cushions and took a sip of her Diet Mt. Dew—the only thing Cami had ever seen her drink besides espresso. "Anyway, I was going to a private school, and the cheer queen was upset the football captain liked me. We had words, which a teacher stopped—*words*, no physical fighting involved. Of course, there may have been slapping and scratching in the future if the teacher hadn't stepped in, but that's beside the point."

Rosemary waved the comment away. "Okay, so I probably would've used my fist, but it never got that far. Anyway, we had a report due for history class, and she copied a paper from the Internet, put my name on it and somehow swapped my actual report. No, I can't prove she was responsible, but," she shrugged, "who else? Then she went to the teacher and said she'd overheard me talking about how I didn't care about the class anyway, and so I'd totally poached a report from online. Of course the teacher did a couple of searches and proved it was stolen. It didn't matter that I had a copy of the report I'd written, the school put me out to dry as an example."

Cami was sure dealing with Rosemary was going to give her ulcers. "You were how old?"

"Seventeen. And I had great self-control. I only keyed her car in response, but I made sure it couldn't be pinned on me, so it's fine." She folded her arms over her chest.

Cami swore. She stood and walked over to the window, fisting her hands to keep from hitting something. Why was she having to deal with this woman? What had her dad been thinking putting Rosemary to work in his hotel?

"Chill, kidding, I didn't key her car. It crossed my mind when I saw it sitting in a parking lot one night, but I held myself back. There is a line."

Cami felt some of the tension eased from her back and shoulders, but kept her hands fisted at her sides as she turned to everyone.

Rosemary rolled her eyes. "Get this woman a shot of something to calm her down before she has a come-apart."

"You know," Cami said evenly, "For someone who lived in Europe for two years, you sure come across as an inner-city delinquent."

Rosemary grinned. "I grew up in D.C. I can be as smooth and cultured as the next person. I just prefer to be myself most of the time."

"Wonderful. Well, we can't do anything about the school expulsion except say it was a misunderstanding, but no one's going to buy it, so let's avoid discussing it at all if possible."

"What do you mean they won't buy it?" Rosemary asked. "It's the truth."

"Doesn't matter. You think people who read these rags care about truth? No, they don't. They care about sensationalism." Seeing Rosemary accept the declaration with bad grace, Cami pushed forward. "Mentioning you completed two full internships in different specialties should go over better. In fact, I think it would be good if we all—including Delphi—wrote up a paragraph or two detailing our professional histories and accomplishments as far as how they prepared us for our roles here. We'll post them up on the website, and create a press release. I'll work with the corporate media specialists and contact Alex to firm things up." They had to do something before this totally got out of control.

The first article had been an irritation; this one took things to a new level.

She stood and moved to the stairs. "Lana, can you contact the others? I'll tweak my own bio. If the past week or two is anything to go by, we need to anticipate more media attacks coming up. If there's anything in any of our pasts that can be dug up or twisted to suit the papers, they'll find it." She glanced back over her shoulders to see Lana's face was white, and Sage's eyes were as big as bagels. Though Cami considered asking what they could possibly be hiding, she didn't have the energy for it.

The night had gone from fabulous to fraught, and Cami

felt wrung out. When she shut the bedroom door, she went through the motions of changing out of her eveningwear into pajamas, doing her facial cleansing and moisturizing routine and sat at the computer. It was too late to call Alex, though she desperately wanted to. He would soothe her and help solve the problem—two things she could use now. She pulled up her bio and made some tweaks to it.

She emailed the PR people at corporate headquarters, directed them to the articles in question—on the off chance they hadn't seen them yet—and copied Alex. Cami mentioned the women would all come up with something to post on the website, and could they please call her at their earliest convenience to discuss strategy.

Though Lana would be the hotel's general manager, it was clear she wanted Cami to deal with the debacle. It was Cami's forte, so she would handle it. It was one more thing to squeeze into her time as she prepared for the hotel opening in seven weeks.

She was already tired.

CHAPTER 18

"Who's behind this, a competitor?" Alex asked when Cami got him on the phone the next day.

"I don't have any reason to believe it is, but it feels too targeted to be run-of-the-mill gossip." Cami sat back in her chair and stretched her aching back.

"I agree. Is there anything else we should be ready to deal with?"

"Who knows? Most of what's been printed was only loosely based on reality. You know how these scandal sheets are." Cami pushed her auburn curls back from her face and thought again of the treadmill downstairs. She ought to have been on it two hours ago, but had spent every moment since she'd woken trying to do damage control. The other inhabitants of the house had already emailed her their bios, and Lana said Delphi would send hers before day's end.

"Normally I wouldn't worry about it, but with all of the negatives blasting back at the hotel, we could be in for some trouble. The reviews of the hotel in the first month and how we handle this will be paramount." A rhythm came through the phone, indicating Alex was tapping his pencil on a notebook—as she'd often seen him do.

"Then we'll make it work, better than work. We'll make it shine."

"I know you will. You ladies make your plans and I'll see if we can figure out where the trouble is coming from."

"Thanks, Alex." Cami said goodbye. She snatched her curls back into a loose ponytail so she could head down to the exercise room. She didn't exercise often, but when her mind was really turning she liked a brisk walk. Some of the others had already done their Zumba DVD and hit the showers, so she should have the space to herself.

She clicked on the news and started walking, letting her mind wander as she moved. Thoughts of her date with Vince the previous night wove in and out of her professional plans, distracting her.

When Cami came out of her room an hour and a half later, fresh from the shower, she heard the doorbell ring and hurried to answer it. Joel stood on the porch, biceps bulging as he crossed his arms. "Hey, I got a call from Alex. He wanted me to stop in and check out your system, make sure everything's extra secure here after the latest news reports."

"Great." Cami used the hand towel to mop at her damp curls. "Go ahead and poke around. I'm not sure how many people are still here, and who's gone down to the hotel, but the recording equipment for the cameras and other security stuff is in the closet off the kitchen." She pointed to the door.

"Perfect. I'll get to it, then." He headed that way and Cami took the stairs to her room.

When she came down again, she found Jonquil sitting at the table, her laptop open. Sage was at the other end of the table reading a book and munching on a bowl of something resembling twigs, with dried cranberries for interest. The woman seriously needed to broaden her food choices.

114

Cami grimaced and headed for the bag of bagels she'd purchased the previous day. She thought nothing of the crinkling sound behind her until Sage spoke up.

"How can you eat that? Don't you know it's loaded with preservatives and stuff?"

Cami turned toward them.

"Leave my *Ho Hos* alone," Jonquil shot back, her mouth already full.

"Rosemary, side with me on this one," Sage said as the chef came down the open staircase.

"*Ho Hos* are the food of the gods," Jonquil stated, stubbornly eating the other half of the first snack cake.

Rosemary came to a stop at the side of the table. "I can't believe we share DNA. You're such a philistine." She grabbed the remaining cake, moved to the sink, and shoved it down the garbage disposal drowning out Jonquil's vibrant arguments. "You'll kill yourself eating those nasty things. It amazes me you can gag them down." She searched through the cupboards.

"I can't believe you did that. Those are mine. And I'm not hoarding a box of them anywhere, so you don't have to go on a search-and-destroy mission. No need for an intervention." The mutinous look on Jonquil's face said she'd like to fight about it. Cami wondered if the memory of Rosemary mentioning her self-defense training held her back.

Rosemary peeked over her shoulder. "That's what you think." She plunked some ingredients onto the cupboard and continued digging. "I have nothing against desserts—I studied with a pastry chef, didn't I? But if you're going to eat them, they should at least taste like actual food. There's no cake flour in this house!" She rooted around some more and moved to the next cupboard.

"*Ho Hos* do taste like actual food. Millions of people eat them every day."

"Yes, and millions of people fill their bodies with illegal drugs, but you wouldn't do it just because they think it's okay." She set a couple more things on the counter and moved to the fridge.

"These aren't illegal."

"They should be," Sage said. "Chemical preservatives have so many drawbacks."

Cami watched in amusement at the byplay. Sometimes living with them reminded her of college dorm life—minus the hunky guys dropping by. She glanced outside and saw Vince's truck pull up, she thought of Joel poking at the security system, and amended her thought. No, this was almost exactly like the dorms.

"No butter? All we have is margarine?" Rosemary turned to Sage. "I thought you were a health nut. How can you put this crap in your body? I thought you were all about natural ingredients."

Sage grinned from where she leaned against the counter on the other side of the island. "I've been getting by with cooking in olive oil, but real butter would be nice."

Rosemary looked at both Sage and Jonquil. "Get your purses and shoes. We're going shopping."

"Busy here," Jonquil crossed her arms over her chest. "And as long as you're going shopping, you can replace my *Ho Hos*."

"Tough. I'm going to teach you a thing or two about buying food. And we'll let Sage tag along, because she probably knows more about the stores and can back me up." Rosemary's blue eyes flashed. "When we get back, I'll show you how pathetic your snack cakes are."

"Actually, Cami's the resident expert about stores and local food sources," Sage said, turning to Cami. "She's been making the rounds."

"I'll pull up the file and print a page for you while you grab your things." Cami checked again and realized it wasn't Vince outside, but one of his employees there to mow the lawn. Disappointment filled her. "I was going to pass it along anyway. I thought you could use some of the local growers to supply the restaurant."

"You betcha. Thanks." Rosemary moved for the staircase ahead of Cami. She shot back over her shoulder to Jonquil, "You're coming with us whether you have shoes on or not. I suggest you find a pair."

Jonquil must have believed the threat since she headed toward her bedroom.

Cami printed her list and handed it to Rosemary as she dragged Jonquil out the door behind her. When Jonquil turned and winked, Cami had to struggle to hold back a laugh at the feigned reluctance until they were out of earshot. She was still grinning when the three of them pulled onto the road in Sage's Ford Fusion.

Looping her purse strap over her shoulder, Cami grabbed her bagel and a bottled orange juice, and headed for her own car. Maybe she'd run into Vince at the hotel.

CHAPTER 19

When Cami arrived at the hotel, she found four guys putting in trays of perennials, but no Vince. She stopped to check out what they were doing. The grounds were going to be beautiful, and she couldn't wait to see how the meandering flowerbeds filled in when the last plants were in place. When Cory, the freckled kid who'd helped with the ballooning adventure, greeted her, she asked, "So where's the boss today? On another property?"

"He's probably still at the nursery digging through paperwork." His grin was quick. "He was grumbling over it when we left there a few hours back."

"Nursery?" Vince worked in a nursery too? Why did he hire out guys to do the work here if he had to have all these extra jobs?

"Yeah, Nature's Garden on Oak Drive."

She paused for a moment. "So how many guys does he have working for him, and are you part time?"

"Full time from the day after school gets out until I go back, part time in the spring and fall, usually. There are about twenty of us on this end of things. Another dozen or so at the nursery." He grinned. "Vince always mutters about tracking inventory and payroll when we ask for a raise, but he's a good boss. Everyone loves him."

The answer gave her pause. So not a small business—at least, not nearly as small as she'd thought. "He owns the nursery, too?"

"Among other things. My mom says he can't keep his fingers out of anyone's pies." He pressed dirt around the plant and rose, collecting the empty plant flats. "I keep thinking I'm going to convince him to take me up in the balloon for free, but he's holding me at the employee discount and working ground crew in exchange for air time. Guess I'm not pretty enough." He chuckled at his own joke and moved to the truck.

Cami considered his words for a couple of seconds before moving back to her car. She pulled up the nursery address and popped it into her phone mapping software before heading off.

Twenty minutes later she found Vince swearing at a computer monitor and riffling through a stack of papers on his desk in what was an otherwise meticulously organized garden center. She shut the office door behind her and stared at him, her arms crossed over her chest and tapping the toe of her Ferragamo pumps.

His expression changed from irritation to happy surprise. "Hey, I didn't expect you to drop by." He rose. The smile dimmed as he approached and he took on a wary expression in his eye. "What's wrong?"

"You have a gnat-sized business? Because thirty-odd employees, even if only for half the year, doesn't seem so gnat sized to me."

He came around the edge of the desk and leaned back against it. "I said compared to the number of employees the hotel was going to be running, it was gnat sized."

"Right. And you're just a small town boy with a good work ethic and big dreams." She'd been had, and she didn't appreciate it in the least. She should have known with a father and two siblings who were lawyers, that Vince wouldn't be content with small potatoes. And hadn't he come across as smooth and educated?

His eyes grew cool. "What's wrong, Cami? Upset I'm not practically a beggar? Harder to blow me off at the end of the summer as a fling—one you indulged in just to get back at your dad—if I'm a real business man?"

"That's not it at all." Except she was starting to wonder if it was. At least partly. She'd thought this was all lighthearted fun and games, and then he ended up being more than she expected. "Tell me, do you have a degree?"

Vince straightened. "I have a master's degree in landscape architecture with a business minor from Cornell." He stepped toward her. "Do you have a problem with that?"

Yes, her mind screamed, but she couldn't admit it. Didn't understand her internal reaction. "I have a problem with being lied to."

"I didn't lie to you. I told you your dad had some dream about us getting together. I told you I owned a business. I'm a landscaper."

"And what other pies do you have your fingers in? I should have known when your dad was such a hotshot lawyer. Your family makes such a pretty picture, all successful and bright and moneyed." She thought about the start-up costs for his business after he attended an expensive university. "Do you have a trust fund, too?" She couldn't *believe* she bought into all of this. Hadn't she learned anything from Trent? No one was what they seemed, were they?

"Don't be a hypocrite, Cami. You're every bit the trust fund baby I am. And more, since I have the funny feeling yours is *far* larger than mine was. And I have my fingers in a few pies. Diversifying is a good bet in a small area like this. Some years the weather doesn't cooperate and we have a bad winter, or a bad snow removal season, or I get a disease blight and lose a bunch of seedlings and have to start over in the spring. It's the whole principle of not putting all your eggs in one basket."

He stepped closer, so there were only inches between them. "And before you ask, yes, I have ties to Gage's ski resort. He, Jeremy, and I have a partnership—if extremely unequal— and that's why I help out with the mountain bike festival and the hot air balloon rides."

She backed into the door as he crowded her, thunder in his eyes, but she kept her head erect and met his gaze. "You've been keeping this from me?"

He raised his hands in disbelief. "If you wanted to know, it's pretty much public record around here. Well, except for the ownership issue at the ski resort. Most people think some big corporation owns it and Gage just manages the thing. It keeps the pressure off some. We admit to the ballooning though."

That didn't make her feel better. "I don't appreciate being made a fool of."

"I don't appreciate you only wanting to be with me if I'm a washed up nobody. You say you're enlightened and don't care about status or money, but then you prove otherwise—

only it's the opposite of what one would expect." He whirled back and returned to his seat. "You can leave now."

"I will. And don't expect to see me back here, either." She pulled the door open and stalked out, refraining from slamming the door behind her.

As soon as she was out of sight, Vince stood and shut the door to give himself some privacy. He swore up a blue streak, kicking at his oak desk, swearing more when it hurt his toes, even through his cowboy boots. He'd never had a woman upset with him for being more successful than she'd first thought.

Things had been going great between them, great conversation, plenty in common, oodles of chemistry. He thought she'd felt the mind-to-mind connection he'd experienced. What was her problem?

When someone came knocking at his office door, he took a calming breath before returning to his chair. "Come in." He had piles of paperwork to catch up on before he could go to a job site and work off his anger with a good sweat. He smiled at the young woman who ran one of his registers and moved back to work mode. There was time to worry about the rest later.

Cami took another survey of the progress at the hotel, and stopped by the local office for the Colorado Department of Labor & Employment to pick up the job applications waiting there. They would do a mass-interview period in three days under Harrison' organized hands, and there would undoubtedly be more interviews to come. They would likely end up interviewing over a thousand people before all of the spots were filled, and she was glad she'd only have to be in on the appointments for her small department, leaving the rest for the others.

Through it all, she thought of her argument with Vince and though she told herself she was in the right, she couldn't let it go.

She returned home to find Rosemary giving Jonquil what was probably an unwanted cooking lesson. Sage sat on the sofa in the great room, setting out lotions and masks, sugar glows and bottles and tubs of things Cami couldn't identify.

Sage smiled at her. "Delphi's catching the red eye and will be here in the morning."

"Great. I've got applications for every department." Cami held up the sheaf she'd picked up, then set them on the kitchen table. "Read them over when you get a minute. Harrison said he'd be here bright and early Saturday to discuss strategy." Retreat was her best option right now, as she didn't think she was fit company, even if she had wanted to spend time with these women—which she didn't.

"As soon as they put the cake in the oven, we're going to test out some new products I'm considering for the spa. Care to join us?" Sage asked.

Cami managed a smile, but couldn't vouch for it coming across happy. "I'm up to my eyebrows in work. But thanks." She hurried away before she could get drawn into more conversation.

As soon as her bedroom door clicked closed behind her, Cami stopped and took a deep breath. She felt so angry. Angry at whomever was causing problems for them in the news. Angry with her father for keeping so many secrets and dumping them all together in this. Angry that he'd planned for her to get together with Vince, and she'd just fallen right into place like the obedient daughter she'd always been. Angry at the other women for existing and ruining her image of the father who had always treated her with the adoration every child deserved.

She didn't have to toe the line in everything, though. And she had no intention of becoming bosom buddies with his other daughters or letting things with Vince get serious. It was time to strike out for independence.

CHAPTER 20

The next morning Cami found hot muffins on the table and Mrs. Grady kneading dough on the counter. "Wow! It smells great."

"Thanks. I thought you girls could use some fresh bread and soup for dinner tonight. I'll finish the cleaning when everyone's gone for the day." Mrs. Grady sprinkled a little more flour onto the counter and returned to kneading. "It sounds like things are getting busy at the hotel."

"There's always something going on," Cami agreed. The hotel itself was only one of her worries. She spotted the plate of chocolate and crème cake rolls Rosemary had made the previous day. They were drizzled with chocolate sauce after the slices had been cut and were to-die-for delicious.

"Looks like one of you girls was busy yesterday," Mrs. Grady commented, seeing Cami study the dessert.

"Rosemary gave Jonquil a lesson on the evils of snack cakes and the joys of cooking." Cami turned her attention back to the split muffin in her hand and spread some jam on it. "If you ask me, Jonquil is still going to sneak in her *Ho Hos*—though the cake rolls are divine." She took a bite of the muffin and made herself a cappuccino.

Mrs. Grady laughed. "My Robert is the same way about those cream-filled oatmeal cookie sandwiches. He says life's too short not to enjoy it while you can." Her smile turned wistful.

"How's he doing?" Cami asked. In all of the craziness of the past few days, she hadn't followed up on the calls she'd made to some friends in Chicago. She would have to take care of that when she reached the hotel.

"He's holding on. We're praying for a donor." Mrs. Grady turned her attention back to her bread, using more force than before.

"I hope it goes well." Cami sat in silence until it was time to leave. What could she say?

Cami sat at the desk in her room Sunday night, typing up notes for the next morning's meeting. She could hear Jonquil's music pounding through her closed bedroom door, and Rosemary called something down the stairs to the others, who were all gathered in the kitchen. Though Cami tried to block it all out, it wasn't easy.

She wished she didn't have to live in this house with so many people. Even in the monstrosity, she could never be alone. Not really. And yet, she didn't feel part of the careful camaraderie they seemed to be developing. Nor did she want to. What was wrong with her, anyway? She had a come apart on Vince, had her world turned upside down, and was forced to live everyday with women whose very presence reminded her George had cheated constantly on her mother. And he kept secrets from her, big, important secrets that affected her after making her trust him with most of her own.

126

Cami thought about taking a trip back to Chicago after the meeting wrapped up the next day. She needed some breathing space. She had a few things in Chicago that needed attention. The break might be perfect.

When she heard a knock at her door, she nearly growled. "Who is it?"

"Lana."

She forced herself to relax. "Come in."

Lana entered and shut the door behind her. "You're always hiding out in here whenever someone else is around."

"It's easier. And quieter. Mostly." She threw a dirty look at the door as another song started on Jonquil's cranked stereo.

Lana managed a half-hearted smile, which worried Cami. She saved her document, then gave her sister her full attention. "What's going on? What's wrong?"

"I wasn't going to tell you." Lana sat on the edge of the bed. "I was never going to tell anyone, but I think maybe . . ." She sighed and rubbed her nose. "I knew Dad was cheating on Mom." She knotted her hands together on her lap, but she held Cami's gaze. "I've known for years."

Cami felt like everything was crumbling around her all over again. "What do you mean? You knew and never told me? Since when? How?"

"I worked with Dad more than you did. Closer. I'd seen the way he checked out other women sometimes. I didn't like it, but I thought, you know, you can't blame someone for looking. He was a guy, after all, even if I didn't like to think of him that way. It was a couple more years before I saw him with someone, saw the way she touched him, the way they couldn't seem to stop staring at each other, and then he kissed

127

her. I almost threw up." She wrapped her arms around her stomach, bending over slightly and her face paled.

"Mom was still alive." Cami was certain—it wouldn't have bothered Lana nearly so much if their mom hadn't still been alive.

"Yes." Lana stood, moving to the window, then back again. "I confronted him, and he denied it. When I told him I knew, that I'd seen him with the bimbo, he told me it was none of my business; he loved Mom but he needed more." She returned to the window, staring out at the lowering sun. "I put in applications everywhere to get away from Dad, was thrilled when the opportunity came up at the Ritz-Carlton."

Cami remembered well her shock that Lana had considered, even for a moment, going to work for someone else. The fact she'd taken the job had been incomprehensible. It hadn't made sense at the time. "You said you wanted to broaden your horizons. You didn't *tell* me." That was one more slap in the face in a growing pile of betrayals she couldn't handle.

"No." She turned back to face Cami, leaning against the window. "At first I couldn't imagine saying it aloud, admitting it, because I was so angry and confused. Then I couldn't tell you because you deserved to be able to think well of him, even if he didn't deserve it. We both thought the sun rose and set with Dad. He wasn't around as much as we'd have liked, and now we know why, but he loved us, talked to us, cheered us on through everything. I didn't want to take that away from you."

Didn't want to take it away from her. What was she, a freakin' china doll? Cami's hands clenched and she set them on her lap, fighting to stay calm. She needed all the answers before she let herself blow up. "What changed your mind? You came back to work for him."

"It was seeing him with Mom when she was sick. He sat by her bedside, hardly ever left it for anything, doted and took care of her, loved her." Lana lifted a hand, shook her head. "No, it didn't make what he did right. Things between us were never the same again. I didn't want them to be—I couldn't trust him anymore. There's no excuse good enough for him to step out on her, and I don't know if I'll ever be able to forgive him for everything he gave to those other women when he should have given it to Mom."

Cami took in the explanation, considered and felt more knotted up inside. "So why are you telling me now?" She wished she didn't know—the last thing she wanted was to be angry at Lana as well. She needed someone she could trust, turn to when everything else was falling down around her.

Lana walked over, picking up Cami's hand. "Because I think sometimes you hold yourself back from the others." She gestured with her head to indicate the women downstairs still kicking up noise and confusion. "Because you still blame them, not for being born, but for knowing something so big when you didn't."

She hurried to clarify before Cami could respond, "I didn't know about the other sisters. He never mentioned it, but I knew he hadn't been faithful, suspected it wasn't a one-time thing, and I never told you. You can't blame them for knowing it, if you don't blame me. They deserve better. You deserve better than holding back from everyone. If we want to make this year anything better than crossing days off a calendar, we need to try being the kind of friends with them that we could have been growing up. Don't discount everyone because your pride has been pricked."

Cami pressed her fingertips between her brows and closed her eyes. She couldn't think. It was too much all at once. "Thanks for telling me."

Silence stretched between them. "Are you okay?"

Was she? Cami didn't know. What did it mean to be okay? She wasn't sure anymore. "I'll be fine. I think I need a drive." She stood, snatching up her car keys. She needed the fresh air blowing against her face, quiet, blessed, impossible-to-find quiet.

"Cami—"

"Please, don't. I need some time to think. Time when I don't have to see the wallpaper Dad picked out for me, or listen to the music pounding through the walls. I need a break. I'll be back later." She snagged her purse and hurried out of the room, leaving Lana standing alone behind her.

CHAPTER 21

Vince walked into the small-town burger joint and got into line to order. It had been a long day—a long several days—while he worked himself to exhaustion. Still, he couldn't get over the betrayal he'd seen in Cami's eyes when he'd told her he wasn't just one step up from a bum.

He rubbed his neck and glanced around to see if he recognized anyone, and stopped short when his eyes landed on Cami.

She sat alone at a window booth, her auburn curls pulled back at the nape of her neck. She wore what she probably thought of as casual clothes—a blouse and dress pants. A burger, fries and shake sat in front of her. Either she'd just gotten them, or she wasn't interested in food, because they'd barely been touched. She had her phone out and studied something on it.

He considered getting his dinner to go, or if he stayed, sitting in the corner where she wouldn't see him. Then she turned and stared out the window at the parking lot, her face reflected back, blank and sad, and he couldn't do it. No matter what she'd thought of him, or what she'd said, he couldn't stand to see that despair. His feelings for her already ran too deep.

As soon as he ordered, he walked over, sitting across from her in the booth. "Hey. Are you still fuming at me?" He'd thought he was mad at her, but he couldn't carry it off. Not right now.

Her eyes closed, making him wonder if she'd known he was there before he'd seen her, or if she was too numb to respond.

"I don't know what I am anymore." She held her breath, her face averted. "What do you want?"

Vince slid a hand over one of hers that sat limp on the table. "Cami, are you okay? Do you need to talk?" He threaded his fingers through hers when she didn't pull away, but she didn't react to his familiarity, either. "Do you want to go somewhere else?"

"Talk?" She shrugged. "What difference would it make?"

They called his number at the front counter. He stood. "I'm going to grab my dinner to go and I'll take you back to my place. You look done in, and we can talk about whatever's on your mind." It worried him, this listless unconcern. It was as if she didn't care what happened. He'd rather see her eyes snapping with anger. When his unilateral decision failed to draw a response from her, he knew it was serious.

He asked the kid at the counter to bag his food and got a cup carrier, packaging Cami's dinner to go as well. When he took her elbow, she grabbed her purse and followed him without argument, climbing into his truck with little encouragement.

Worry zinged through him and he wondered if she was physically sick and not just upset. As soon as he pulled onto the road, he asked. "Is someone hurt? Are you ill? Have there been more articles? What's wrong?"

She shrugged. "Nothing and everything." A tear trickled down her cheek.

He hated when women cried. Nothing panicked him like tears. "Hey, don't. You can't cry over nothing. You said it was nothing." He pushed harder on the gas, anxious to get home, racking his brain, trying to come up with some way to stop the tears.

He was grateful his house was close as he pulled the truck into the driveway and tossed it into park. He hurried around to her side, opening the door, but she just sat there. "Come on, baby, do you hear the dogs? They know I'm home and are getting worked into a frenzy."

When he tugged on her hand, Cami followed after him, bringing her purse and the burgers as he asked her to, but she still didn't speak. She wiped at a tear streaking down her cheek and sniffled.

"The dogs are shut in the back yard. They won't knock you over, no matter how much they want to." They could wait a few minutes. He found himself jabbering nonsense, hoping it would stop her tears. He set the food on the kitchen counter, stashed their shakes in the freezer, and led her back to the living room, sitting beside her on the sofa. "Okay, tell me what happened."

"Nothing. Nothing happened." Sniff. "Nothing new; just new to me. Why does it all have to change?" The tears came fast and fevered now and Vince hurried to scrounge up the box of tissues his mother had brought him when he had the flu. He pressed a wad into her hands and pulled her into his chest. She snuggled there as if she belonged, felt right in his embrace. He pushed the thought away, focusing on what she needed instead.

133

Cami started to talk, babbling as much as anything, but he was able to piece it together. He learned only a small part of her doldrums had to do with their confrontation three days earlier. He caught bits about music on too loud, people everywhere, Lana keeping secrets, George betraying them all, and the inevitable accusations that he'd lied and let her think he was a regular guy.

He wondered what she'd think if he told her he *was* a regular guy. A degree from Cornell and his various business interests didn't take away the fact that he worked hard with his hands every day, that he'd rebuilt his car engine twice with the help of friends, or that the feel of her in his arms, even weepy and blowing her nose, did things to his system.

He soothed and patted and whispered nonsense, doing anything he could think of to calm her. The sobbing stopped, the shaking slowed, and her hand slid from where it had rested on his chest to trace his collar bone, up the side of his neck, and along the side of his jaw. Her scent surrounded him, the silkiness of her skin made him hyper aware of their proximity. When she tipped her face up to him, he found himself drawn to the offer of her lips. He'd been aching to hold her for days, to clear the air between them. Though there was still too much left unspoken, he took what she offered and gave it back in return.

The kiss started soft and tentative, but grew in strength until it became something else entirely. He lost himself in the kiss, in the wicked fluidity of her mouth, the eagerness with which she dove into it. That was, until he realized she was tugging on his T-shirt.

Though just being close to her threw his libido for a loop, and the movement of her hands on his chest made it all worse, he covered her hands and stopped them. He kissed her for a moment more before he was able to slow it down, then finally pull back, his better judgment kicking in against his preferences. "Whoa, slow down, honey. Slow down." She was not in any place emotionally to make those kinds of decisions and they had too many misunderstandings between them to go there tonight. When her lips landed on his neck and she hummed against his skin, it was all he could do to keep his resolve. "Hold off, sweetheart. You don't want to do that right now. Come on." He shifted back, his hand on her shoulders.

Her fists clenched and she pushed away, pushed him. "How do you know what I want or don't want? Who died and made you king?" She stood, but drilled a sharp finger into his chest. "Just because Daddy approved of you doesn't make you my keeper."

"I never said it did. Gees, that hurts!" He grabbed her hand so she would stop poking him. "Calm down." But he was relieved to see the show of temper. It was much easier to deal with Cami mad than weepy or half comatose.

"Don't tell me to calm down. Do you think I like having people run my life for me? First Lana finds out about Dad's *extracurricular* activities, and decides to keep it to herself. Then after he dies I learn about my four extra sisters; he does his utmost to turn my life upside down—have you ever lived with five women? I'm telling you, even with our own rooms and bathrooms, it's not a pretty sight. And that's with Mrs. Grady coming in to clean up and make a meal three times a week. What are we, anyway, helpless?" She gave his shoulder a shove, though there wasn't much heat behind it.

"No, of course not." He didn't know what else to say. Not everything she said made sense, but her actions were helping him clear his mind and focus on the issues between them.

"And," she went on as if he hadn't spoken, "Dad starts pulling strings to get us together, putting a bug in your ear about how much *alike* we are, making you wonder what's wrong with me. I think you're this strong, sexy, hardworking type who's absolutely nothing like the last guy I dated—though you're exactly the kind of guy he threatened I'd end up with, or at least I thought you were. He was sure I'd catch a loser in the end, and you didn't end up being one, and Lana decides it's time to come clean about knowing about Dad for *years*."

"Hold on," Vince interrupted, fury racing through him. "What do you mean I didn't end up being a loser? You said you didn't think your dad would like me, but you didn't say you thought I was a *loser* when you agreed to join my family for the Fourth. You have a lot of nerve. Nobody's slumming when they go out with me."

She took a step back, held up her hands, took a slow breath. "No kidding. I'm sorry, that's not what I meant."

"So what did you mean?" He stood to face off with her. How could he have such strong feelings for someone who thought he was a loser?

She turned away and raked both hands through her curls and he realized she'd lost her elastic at some point. After a moment, she turned back, much calmer. "I didn't think you were a loser. You had a steady job, and Dad had hired you, so you obviously knew what you were doing. He didn't suffer fools. I just . . . I thought I was getting away from his maneuvering. And then it turned out I fell right back into his plans when we started dating. You were exactly the guy he wanted for me, the one I've searched for, despite the slightly different packaging than I'd expected."

"What's wrong with my packaging?" The fury was gone, but confusion and irritation were still wildly abundant. Did

136

she realize she'd said he was what she wanted? Had he imagined it?

She looked him up and down. "Oh, nothing, I promise."

For some reason her frank appraisal embarrassed him and he set his hands on his hips as the anger and irritation deserted him. "So what's the deal?"

She turned and paced across the room, then came back. "I don't know what to do with you, Vince. I don't know what to do with myself when I'm around you, and I feel things for you I've never felt before, and that scares the crap out of me."

He rubbed his stomach where her words had sent his insides twisting. "Well, now we're even." When she lifted an inquiring brow, he clarified. "I've had relationships, but there was no falling in love. Attraction, the excitement that comes at the beginning of a new relationship, yes, but not love—if that's what I'm even feeling. I'm not sure I'm ready to deal with all of this so soon."

The woman had to be schizophrenic or something to flip flop from one emotion to the next so fast. He was going to get whiplash if she didn't slow down. But was he any better? His anger had never peaked and melted away so fast before.

"I guess there's no rush." She let out a shaky breath and forced a smile. "How about if we reheat those burgers and eat. I'm starved."

"Okay, fine." Bewildered, he followed her through the house to the kitchen.

CHAPTER 22

When the food was in the microwave, Vince opened the back door and his two dogs shot into the room, barking like mad, running in circles, and jumping up on Cami in delight. He gave each of them a firm patting, then yanked them back onto all fours when they nosed at the milkshakes on the counter. The monsters were big as horses and ate twice as much—each. "All right, get down and I'll get you two some food."

He crossed to the closet and pulled out a huge scoop to ladle kibble into the metal doggie bowls. Then he grabbed a gallon pitcher and topped off their water bowls inside and out. When he came back, Cami was seated at the table, both dogs quivering at her feet, their eyes filled with hope as she unwrapped her burger.

"Don't turn your back on them," he warned her, "or your food will disappear in one gulp."

"You just fed them."

"Doesn't matter. They're bottomless pits." Still, he gave each of their heads an affectionate rub, then washed his hands before he sat with his food.

They ate in silence for a few minutes before he broached the subject he'd been turning over in his mind. "So what's the big problem here? Is it that your father managed to manipulate your life, even from the grave? Is it the pressure you're getting from the media?" She eyed him and he shrugged. "I've been paying attention."

She was thoughtful as she chewed and swallowed. "I've never told anyone this before." She dipped her fry in her shake, swirled it around, and ate it while the suspense increased. "About four years ago I dated a guy named Lance. We went out for several months. I was starting to think maybe there was a future for us. I thought we fit so well and had so much in common. Then one day I was working at the hotel, doing paperwork from the front desk when a woman came to speak with me." Cami paused as she picked out a pickle hanging from the burger. "She asked me to stop seeing her husband."

Vince's throat closed up on him as he watched the emotions flit through her face, so many, too fast to capture.

"I was the other woman, Vince. We weren't sleeping together, but I was still keeping him from his family."

"No." He reached over and wrapped her fist in his hand. "You weren't doing it. You didn't know, did you?"

"No. I didn't know. I sent him a text message telling him not to bother me again. He only made a token attempt to convince me to keep seeing him. I've only run into him once or twice at social events since, but he took me at my word and has never done more than greet me in passing. I've seen him with other women he's dated, and yet he's never divorced his wife."

"You don't understand that." He understood better how deep her rage and confusion went.

"She never left him, and she probably never will." She

lifted wet eyes to his. "Did my mom know? Did she put up with it all those years, knowing there were legions of other women? Why would she do that?"

He took her hand, flipping it over to rub his thumb across her palm. "Maybe things changed by the time you were old enough to remember. There are only what, four, five years between you and Jonquil?"

Her eyes closed in pain. "Barely four. But he didn't change. Lana told me tonight, she saw him with another woman a couple of years before my mom died. When Lana confronted him, he said it was none of her business. Yet he still acted so devoted to Mom, put everything aside to be with her when she was sick." She shook her head. "I just can't figure out how to fit all of the puzzle pieces back together in a way that makes sense."

He wished he could take away her pain, and was left feeling powerless. "How do your sisters feel about it?"

She shrugged one shoulder. "Lana feels the same pull between loving him and not wanting to forgive him."

Seeing she wasn't going to volunteer more, he prodded her. "And the others?"

Cami pulled her hand out of his and took a bite of her hamburger, seeming to mull the thought over while she chewed and swallowed. "I haven't asked. It's too hard to be around them. Lana said I blame them for knowing Dad was . . . playing the field before I knew. That's not it, though. It's the anger and despair, the sadness and loss of trust in my own ability to make good decisions that I felt when I learned Lance was married.

"Their mothers had to have gone through the same thing. Most of his other daughters probably had their own period of disillusionment, and if I'm going to be close to them, I have to accept it. It's hard knowing he hurt so many people. And if those women knew he was married and saw him anyway, it only makes it worse."

Unable to help himself, Vince leaned over, slid his fingers behind her neck and pulled her close so he could touch his lips to her forehead. "It's never easy, is it?"

"No." She lifted her gaze to his. "I keep thinking it ought to be easy, but it's not. What kind of father could he have been to them, scattered across the country, when he spent so much time in Chicago?"

"Maybe you should ask."

Cami smiled in greeting as they filed into Blake's office the next morning. All six sisters surrounded the conference table he'd squeezed into the room.

"Sorry, this table will eventually end up in the room next door, but the room's not ready, so you'll have to deal with the tight quarters today. Once this place opens, I know Lana intends to hold her daily staff meetings around it, so we'll have plenty of opportunity to grow familiar with it." He smiled easily at the group, which included Joel, who had arrived before the ladies.

Blake focused on Lana, who sat around the corner from him on the long table. "My apologies for usurping your place. That seems to happen when we meet in my office, a problem that will soon be rectified. Please, go ahead." He slid into his seat.

Lana's face tightened and she met his gaze directly, her hands folded primly on the table top. "You're the regional manager. It's in your purview to lead the meeting when you're around."

"But I'll be available for a great deal more of these meetings than I would if my office were located elsewhere, so I'd prefer to let you run the meeting. Just leave me a spot on the timetable in case I have anything to discuss. Go ahead." There was challenge in his eyes.

Cami watched for and saw the answering challenge in Lana as her back grew even straighter, though Cami wouldn't have thought it possible.

"Thank you. We'll get on with it. Today's company message first." She imparted the daily corporate message shared at staff meeting at all of the hotels every morning. She had Blake give the updates on the construction and orders that had been submitted, asking for information from others at the table, starting with Rosemary on her left.

They each took their turns discussing their plans and ideas, mentioning any difficulties they were having. Joel discussed security issues before Lana brought up another issue. "I don't suppose any of you have seen the latest on the Star Gazing website, since it hasn't been mentioned yet." She named a gossip publication notorious for making up things when they didn't have truth to publish.

"What are you talking about?" Cami asked as her stomach twisted.

Lana's gaze slid over everyone in the room. "They've taken their jabs at me. I'm not sure if it could have been worse or not."

Cami asked, "What about you? What could they have possibly found on you? You're like Mrs. Clean."

Lana's eyes slid to Blake's, and he lifted a brow, almost

appearing amused. Her mouth twisted for a moment before she explained. "They found pictures of me drunk the day I turned twenty-one. It was part celebration, part drowning my sorrows as I had learned only a few days earlier that Dad was cheating on my mom. Photos can be doctored, but the ones in the article are the way I remember it. Fuzzy."

Blake frowned, but lifted a hand to her shoulder, giving it a squeeze. She shrugged it off and kept her face unreadable. "Most everyone has had a moment of weakness where they made mistakes," he soothed. "This is hardly news. I'd say a drinking binge on the twenty-first birthday is pretty common."

"The problem," Cami pointed out, "since you're so young, people will question the soundness of having you in charge. I'm sorry to say it, because you know I think Dad was right to put you where you are, but people like to talk."

"So no wine for you at dinner if we're in public. No problem," Rosemary said airily.

"I don't know that we need to go that far, she is almost thirty," Blake said, but asked Lana, "I'm assuming you got a cab, or used a designated driver?"

"Of course. My boyfriend at the time chose to stay sober to make sure I got home okay." Her voice turned almost sickly sweet. "*He* was so thoughtful."

Blake's eyes shuttered. "Then you should be fine. Drinking responsibly and everything."

"There are only pictures of me with a margarita, so nothing particularly damning." Lana glanced back at the room. "Is there anything else we need to discuss, or do we adjourn the meeting?"

When no one said anything, Cami moved to adjourn and

they all agreed. When they stood to leave, however, Blake kept Lana back, shutting them into his office while the rest tromped downstairs.

CHAPTER 23

That evening while the sisters sat around the table enjoying one of Mrs. Grady's fabulous dinners, Cami was surprised when Lana brought up the issue of the opening party.

"Why didn't we discuss this during our earlier meeting?" Cami asked.

Lana's eyes narrowed. "While Dad had plans in place for the grand opening gala, and Blake's been finalizing them, he asked me this afternoon to get your feedback on the big promotional thing they're going to announce next week." She pulled out some papers. "He's on the plane to California now, so I'll send him a report with our thoughts, and copy the corporate PR people, but I thought we could toss around some ideas tonight."

Delphi sat back, her usual skinny latte cupped between her hands. "So what do they have planned so far?"

"PR is already working on a campaign to give away some stays the weekend of the gala, starting with two four-night, major packages. It'll be for one of the nicer suites, with meals and spa treatments—"

Cami interrupted. "Throw in a hot air balloon ride. If we

can't get the ski resort to donate it, I should at least be able to broker a discount, since they'll get extra publicity in the campaign. It's seriously incredible." Vince had promised to take her up again as soon as the hotel had opened and she had time to breathe again. She couldn't wait.

Delphi shivered. "No one is getting me three-thousand feet off the ground in a wicker basket, thank you very much. Just the thought freaks me out."

"We can include those bedtime snack trays for two of the four nights, or one of those rose petal bed treatments," Rosemary suggested.

Lana typed more notes. "Great. Any other ideas?"

They threw around thoughts for the packages and discussed the grand opening gala. Dessert was long gone when the conversation wound down and Lana turned off her computer.

"So where did you go last night?" Jonquil asked Cami. "You were gone for hours. I heard you sneak in."

Cami played with the water bottle she'd switched to after her dessert coffee. She almost hadn't stayed for chat after the unofficial meeting, but her conversation with Vince the previous night had left her with questions only the other daughters could answer. "I drove around for a while. Stopped in at a burger place for dinner and Vince walked in. We talked, and he took me back to his place to eat and stuff."

"And stuff?" Rosemary's voice was infused with meaning.

Though she tried to keep her expression cool, her lips quirked when she shot Rosemary what was supposed to be a quelling glance. Talking about her relationship was new to her and made her uncomfortable, though thoughts of Vince made her insides tingle. "It was talk. And some kissing." She grinned. "Okay, a lot of kissing, and some crying on his shoulder. The man's a saint for putting up with me. And for sticking my shake in the freezer so I didn't come back to Oreo crumbs drowning in chocolate cream."

"You cried on him? What did he do?" Sage asked. "My brother can't stand it when I cry. He ends up giving me anything I want." She frowned into her herbal tea. "Of course, not every guy is like that. I can't see muscle man security expert Joel giving anyone what they want, for any reason. I swear the man's a robot."

Cami thought the description of Joel was very apt. "Vince was sweet, very sweet, and we hashed out a lot of the stuff that's been bothering me." She shot an apologetic look at Lana, feeling guilty. "Sorry I didn't talk it over with you. You're just so mixed up in all of this, I needed an impartial listener."

"And it didn't help when I dropped my own bombshell on you," Lana agreed.

"Oh? Do tell," Rosemary set aside her espresso cup. The woman lived on the potent brew—and way later into the night than Cami would ever consider.

Lana pushed her fiery locks back from her face, glanced around the group. "I caught Dad cheating about eight years ago, when I was still in hotel management school. When I confronted him, it wasn't pretty. Then I went to work at Ritz-Carlton for a while. I'm glad to have the experiences I had with them, but I didn't do it to broaden my horizons—I did it because I was angry and needed some space. I never said anything to Cami, and she wasn't very happy about it." Her gaze centered back on Cami. "I'm sorry I unloaded on you last night."

It still hurt, but she was starting to get a handle on it. "It was time you told me, and you had a good point, or three." Cami sipped at the water and considered the discussion she'd had with Vince. She hesitated, then plunged ahead. "I have a question for the rest of you. You were spread out all over the place, and Dad was home close to half the time. I know he traveled a lot, but what kind of father was he to you? You couldn't have seen much of him."

Jonquil was the first to answer. "We spoke on the phone at least twice a week—every week—for as long as I can remember, and though I never saw him on holidays, there was always a special gift, an extra phone call. He made it to my birthday dinners a few times over the years. I saw him at least every other month. I always wished it could be more, but it was still better than lots of my friends who had divorced parents."

"Same here," Rosemary stated. "Except for my time abroad, when we cut back on visits, but he still called, kept in touch."

"He always called," Sage agreed. "But there was a long stretch when I wouldn't talk to him." She looked at Lana, then Cami. "Right after I found out about you guys, that I was between you in age, I stopped taking his calls. He'd been my hero, and I didn't like learning he had feet of clay." She wore a wistful smile. "When he came for his scheduled visit, I yelled and screamed at him, I pounded on his chest, and told him what I thought of the way he used my mom, the way he neglected his wife and kids because of me.

"He held me and told me he loved me until I calmed down. Finding out our moms weren't isolated incidents hasn't been all butterflies and cotton candy for us either." She said this last straight out to Cami, making her feel ashamed that she'd been acting as if she were the only injured party.

Sage wet her lips and brushed the dark curls behind her ear. "Dad and my mom had no relationship besides sharing me since shortly after I was conceived, but he was around as much as he could be. He always made sure I had money for special extras, even when Mom married a few years later. He didn't want me to go without things he thought I should have, and he treated my brother Harrison the same way, though without the special phone calls and daddy-daughter dinners."

"That would have been a stretch for him and Harris to do the daddy-daughter thing. Funny, though." Rosemary's grin didn't dim when Sage threw a decorative pillow at her.

"He always made time to do what interested me and he nurtured my dreams, encouraged me to do what made me happy, even if it wasn't what he valued." Delphi grimaced. "There were lots of times I felt second place to you two, but that was because he didn't acknowledge me in public rather than because he didn't make a real effort to keep up on what was going on in my life."

"If I wanted to talk, needed to vent, whatever, he always made time, even if it wasn't our scheduled talk time," Rosemary added. "And if he was in a meeting, he always called back within a few hours. He never forgot or blew me off."

"There's no question we all wish he'd been around more." Jonquil said. "But considering how many of us there are, and the geographical problems, I'm impressed he managed so well. But I guess he always had the excuse of checking in on the resorts where we lived."

Tears started pouring down Cami's cheeks and she brushed them away. He really had loved them all, and made sure they felt it. Knowing this only confused her more as she tried to piece together the man she'd thought she knew with these new facets of his personality. "Thank you. This has been a lot to take in, and I don't know how to deal with it."

"You're not the only one who feels that way," Jonquil pointed out. "Even though we knew about you, we didn't know about each other, and Dad had an amazing ability to maneuver everyone around him to do his bidding." Her jaw set at a surly angle.

"You're not kidding. I still can't believe Delphi and I were on the same floor of the dorm and never had a real conversation." Cami asked Delphi, "Did you know then?"

Delphi nodded. "Yeah. And I recognized you the first day I moved in. I was curious about you, even while I resented you for being the one he acknowledged. Did you notice he never came to the campus or dorms that year?"

Cami paused and thought back, then snorted in disgust. "You're right. I never thought about it, though. He didn't want to run into one of us while he was with the other one." She called him a harsh name.

Rosemary laughed, but Sage gave Cami an admonishing glare.

Cami debated mentioning more, and decided to come clean. "He put a bug in Vince's ear about me while they were planning the landscaping. He had Vince thinking I must have been a wallflower or something for Dad to be so pushy about how I was perfect for him, but it got him to step up and learn more about me." She swore. "I actually thought I was making my own moves on this relationship, and then it turned out he'd manipulated that, as well."

"He didn't manipulate you into accepting a date, though," Jonquil pointed out. "You did it on your own. And weren't you dating someone pretty recently?"

150

"Ah, yes, Trent. The sludge of humanity. I split with him in January when I realized he was searching for a cash infusion. He kept popping back up, trying to convince me to give him another chance after Dad died. I guess our relationship *was* pretty well known. Too bad his financial need wasn't quite as clear when we started dating." She still couldn't believe she'd been so gullible.

"So you split with him because he wasn't as rich as you?" Rosemary asked.

"No." Cami infused ice into her voice at the suggestion. "I dumped him because he cared more about the money than about me. I'm not giving a fortune hunter the time of day."

"But did you care about him?" Jonquil asked.

Cami set her water to the side and shifted in her spot. "Not as much as I thought at the time." She waved a hand. "Oh, I felt betrayed, but mostly I was embarrassed I let myself be taken in. Letting him go was ridiculously easy."

"That's almost harder," Jonquil said with a nod. "I split with my boyfriend of two years, just realized it wasn't going anywhere. I think I was more upset it took me so long to realize there wasn't anything between us and we'd wasted our time than I was at the split." She smiled. "Dad always said he was too bland for me. It's irritating when you find out he's right."

"Isn't it, though?" Rosemary asked. "Well, if Dad was in the matchmaking business for us before he died, no way am I going to start up anything with a guy he knew. Better yet, I'll be far too busy running my kitchen to get involved with any guy at all for the next year, at least."

Cami decided it was time for a change of subject. "Any interesting applicants in the pile I brought home?"

151

"A few, and a few others I'll check into for servers and stuff. The applications better keep pouring in, because no way could we staff the entire hotel from what we've seen, and there were definitely a few I wouldn't consider interviewing, never mind hiring."

Cami grinned. "I've been in touch with a concierge from the Four Seasons in Denver. She thinks she might like a change of scene, and she'd be a great resource as we're starting out. I've known her for a few years. She's *very* good." If she managed to get Lorna, it would make her life so much easier.

"That would be a coup," Lana agreed.

"Yes it would."

They took turns discussing hiring possibilities, then directed the subject elsewhere. Cami mostly sat back and listened to the banter as it flowed from one woman to the next. She hadn't considered the others might be struggling as much with current events as she was, or that they might be angry and confused about why their dad had kept so many secrets. They'd all lost something when their father died. But maybe, just maybe, the note he'd left her, his words about wanting her to have her sisters there to love and support her, would be fulfilled after all. Eventually.

CHAPTER 24

Vince smiled when he found Cami gathered around the island with her sisters, putting together sandwiches for dinner. "Hey, a room full of beautiful women, what more could a man want?"

"Join us for dinner." Cami accepted his peck on the lips, warming him with her smile.

"I think I will." He pulled her into a hug and leaned against the counter, enjoying the babble of women's voices, and more importantly, the feel of Cami in his arms after a long day of slogging through paperwork at the nursery.

The door to the garage opened and Delphi came through in one of her sleek suits. She pointed at Vince, irritation on her face. "Your friend is the most arrogant ass I've ever met."

"Things didn't go well with Jeremy?" Cami asked.

"Wait, Jeremy's the ass? What did he do?" Jeremy was usually so good with women, and Delphi so professional, he must have really done something out of character to get her fuming.

She dumped her attaché in a chair in the great room and stormed back to him on three-inch heels. "I'd known him all of thirty seconds when he made some arrogant statement about how he wasn't interested in marriage no matter how much I was worth. As if I were some wannabe contestant for The Bachelor or something. As if I didn't already have a boyfriend and actually cared what the jerk wanted."

Vince tried to choke back a laugh, but couldn't manage it. "He's usually very smooth with beautiful women. I don't know what he was thinking." Vince *did* know what Jeremy had been thinking, but obviously George hadn't shared his grand plans for his daughters' marriages with the ladies. "What did you say?"

She told them about Jeremy insisting she'd been checking him out, and her rebuttal that it was the bike she was interested in. When she said she'd told Jeremy his bike was way hotter than he was, Vince barely managed to hold back the guffaw that ached to explode.

"Is it true?" Jonquil asked. "Is the bike way hotter?"

Delphi eyed Vince. "You ever repeat what I'm about to say, and I'll make sure you pay for a long, long time." When he held up his hands in defense, she grinned at Jonquil. "Oh, the bike is super-hot, and the guy is a pretty good match. Too bad his personality hotness quotient dropped like fifty points when he opened his mouth."

"Too bad." Jonquil piled a handful of chips on the side of her plate. "What did you think of his work?"

"Top notch. I guess I'll deal with the arrogance." She looked at Sage. "I don't know how you put up with him on the Fourth of July."

"He had a girl with him, and I wasn't checking out his...equipment, so apparently he didn't see a point in going on the offense," Sage said with a teasing smile. "Besides, you might change your mind about him later."

Delphi snorted. "Not likely."

Wishing he hadn't promised to keep this exchange to himself, Vince decided having the sisters around could be very entertaining.

"Joel, don't think you're getting out of this," Sage called out as the sisters collected in the entrance to the hotel.

Cami laughed when he pulled a face. The entire executive staff was getting their pictures taken and Joel had done nothing but scowl and complain since the announcement was made. The sisters were all in professional outfits of one kind or another—though Rosemary wore a chef's uniform, and Sage wore the polo and dress pants that were her typical spa uniform.

"I can't believe you're wearing that, and I'm in a dress suit," Jonquil complained. "I should never have let Delphi help me pick something."

"Blue is your color and the pictures are going to be awesome," Delphi said, adjusting the collar on her blouse.

Jeremy stood by in jeans, a tight white tee and his signature sunglasses. His camera, a tripod and a long pole were all strapped to him as he watched the group of women with thinly disguised irritation. "Are we about ready?"

"I'm not wearing a suit coat," Joel stated as he came to join the group.

"You're fine the way you are." Rosemary smoothed a wrinkle in the green polo he wore that had the company logo and his name embroidered on it. "You just need to seem tough and intimidating. See there, you've already got it down." •

Cami held in a chuckle. Joel hadn't changed his usual expression one iota.

When she realized he was staring at someone walking into the building, Cami turned to the man approaching them. He grinned broadly and offered her his hand. "Hi, you'd be Camellia, right?"

"Yes, have we met?"

"I'm Larry Clonger, a reporter with—"

That was as far as he got before Joel stepped in and started herding the man back to the outside door. "If you want interviews, you'll have to go through proper channels," he said.

"But I wanted to ask the ladies about the rumors that have been cropping up," the reporter protested.

"Then call and set something up. Now isn't a good time." Joel lifted his radio and called for backup before he got out of hearing. "They're very busy getting ready for the resort opening."

"That was interesting," Rosemary said, straightening her uniform.

"They're coming out of the woodwork. Joel and the other security guys are already working overtime to keep the reporters at bay and screen incoming calls," Lana said with a sigh.

"It'll blow over soon. We're really not that big of news," Jonquil said.

"Yeah, until someone finds or makes up something spectacular enough to print again." Lana frowned.

"You have something to hide?" Rosemary asked, her brows lifting suggestively.

Blake came down the stairs and joined them "Sorry I'm late. Where do you want us?" he asked Jeremy.

They went out to a nice spot in the landscaping with rocks and trees and Jeremy started ordering people around. Delphi kept things moving along, not letting time lapse between pictures, while Lana ensured everyone's clothes were smooth and hair perfect for each shot.

Jeremy had all of the sisters get together for a group picture. "Don't you want everyone in this?" Cami asked.

"We'll take one in a minute, but for this picture we're going to focus on the idea of family running the hotel, a family you trust and believe in," Jeremy said. "That's what the PR person said."

"So what am I doing here?" Joel asked.

Sage gave him a saucy smile. "You'll live."

"Jeremy, is the picture balanced? Maybe I should switch with Jonquil," Delphi said as she touched her hair.

"It's fine. This is my job. You can trust me to do it right, your majesty."

Delphi sent him a quelling look, then put on a smile and posed for the shot.

CHAPTER 25

The sisters came and went over the next weeks as their schedules demanded, but by August first everyone was in residence fulltime. Cami forced herself to join the others for after-dinner conversations, movie nights and even did a few Zumba sessions with them—in which she learned that yes, Delphi was every bit as uncoordinated as she claimed.

Most of the rooms in the hotel had been completed. Furniture and supplies were arriving by the trailer load—which had them all working long hours training new employees and seeing everything put in place.

Then one evening Lana came out of her bedroom, stood at the top of the stairs, and yelled out that there was an emergency meeting, and everyone better get their tails in the great room pronto.

Cami grabbed her laptop and joined the ladies in the comfy seats around the coffee table, which Jonquil loaded up with sodas, a hot pot of coffee and munchies.

"What is that all for?" Delphi asked.

"Brain food. If this is an emergency meeting, I thought snacks might be in order." Jonquil pulled out a package of Godiva chocolates and arranged them alongside the rest.

"Now you're talking," Rosemary said as she grabbed one.

Lana was grim faced. "Now that we don't have to worry about starving, can we get down to business?"

"If this is a business meeting, shouldn't we be holding it at the hotel?" Delphi asked.

"We're all here, so Blake is on his way to join us," Lana said. "He'll have all the details, but the fact is, we've had another media hit, and it's going to cost us in the pocketbook big time. And more if word gets out."

"If it's an article, I don't see how we could possibly keep it quiet," Sage said. She pulled her feet up onto the sofa beneath her, leaving her sandals on the floor.

"What's going on?" Cami asked.

Lana peered at her computer screen. "It's in the Market News."

Confidence in the Six DiCarlo Daughters Wanes as the Opening Date of the Latest Resort Approaches

The DiCarlo Hotel chain has received a fresh infusion from the family line since George DiCarlo's death, but confidence in his daughters has waned and stock in his company has hit an all-time low.

"There's still plenty of time to see what his daughters make of the newest resort in the chain," Vice President Clark Thomas of DiCarlo Hotels, Inc said. "I wouldn't count them out yet. The proof is in the pudding, as they say."

The opening date for the new resort grows ever closer and rumors of security problems, late deadlines and unfinished projects abound.

With an executive staff made up almost entirely of inexperienced family members, many worry nepotism will be the downfall of this venture.

"Oooh, that's slander," Jonquil said when the room had been silent for a long moment.

"Libel, but it actually toes the line very closely. There's nothing absolutely false in the article. Alex said they'd take a look at suing them," Lana said with a grimace.

"More bad news," Cami continued. "Less than an hour ago I received an email from the reservations department. The prince of Denmark and his entourage have canceled their reservations for January, citing concern about their security while on site."

"That's ridiculous, as if they weren't bringing a phalanx of their own staff, in addition to the super-tight restrictions Joel was going to run while they were here," Sage argued.

"Yeah, but apparently they weren't interested in reassurances or discussing security in more detail." Lana's face was grim.

"It gets worse," Delphi said. "Well, no, nothing's worse than losing the prince as a client, but we have an additional snag. The Buehler wedding has been cancelled. Or rather, it's been moved to an alternate location. I was on the phone with the mother for over an hour this afternoon, offering almost everything from discounts to a free cake."

Rosemary glowered at her. "You're not giving away one of my cakes. They're works of art."

"Art everyone eats," Delphi said.

"Once it's been appreciated and photographed, that's

fine—cake is meant to be eaten." Rosemary folded her arms over her chest. "It's still art."

"I offered her an equivalent price break on the package, which she turned down despite some serious temptation. The only thing she didn't have a problem with is Jeremy's photography skills. Apparently *he's* good enough." Her tight mouth broadcast her take on that. "Then again, her future son-in-law went to school with Jeremy, they were buddies, and he couldn't possibly dump Jeremy too—not when so much of the work had already been put in."

"Let's forget the hours you've spent with her on details, I've put in on cake design, Jonquil has spent discussing flowers," Rosemary said with a twist of her mouth.

"Of course, those details are so minor and our time isn't worth anything to her." Delphi shot Rosemary a grin. "Don't worry. She isn't getting her deposit back, and they'll be paying penalties as well. But it's not a good omen if the locals won't even use us."

The doorbell rang and Lana rose to answer it. Blake strode in wearing jeans and a T-shirt, which was the most casual thing Cami had ever seen him wear. "Hey, ladies." He took a glance around at the food piled on the table. "I can always get behind a meeting that includes food." He took an empty spot—the one next to Lana's laptop—and grabbed a Coke.

Though Lana shot him a dirty look, she moved the laptop and sat beside him.

"So have you filled everyone in?" he asked.

"Yes, plus apparently we had a wedding cancellation."

Delphi gave a short explanation.

161

"Well, it seems like we need to do more about the bad press. Any ideas?"

Lana looked at Cami. "There's the Franklin's summer party. The prince's cousin almost always attends, as do several others with whom you are far friendlier than I am."

The thought of being stuck for a full evening at the stuffy affair when she could be here with Vince made Cami's teeth grind. "Yes, but you're the hotel manager, I'm a lowly serf in comparison."

"Give me a break. You have the golden touch with people. We need you to go rub elbows with a few of them. In addition, I'll send a note to the prince's secretary expressing our disappointment about the miscommunication and offering to put up his representative for a few days at no cost so they can review protocols and safety measures on location. It may net us nothing, but it can't hurt."

"Both good suggestions." Blake turned to Delphi. "Is there anything we can do about the wedding?"

"I'm not sure I want to deal with them after all of this," she said, but she twisted a pen between her fingers. "They said the groom is friends with Jeremy. Maybe he's also friends with Vince?" she smiled at Cami, hopefully.

When did this all become her mess? "Oh no, I'm not asking him for that kind of favor. You can stop that train of thought right there."

"I'm not saying he should step up and try to convince them this is the best place, the only place. I just think some schmoozing might be in order. You know, he gets together with friends and you happen to be there. Isn't there some barbecue coming up? You two discuss the way the landscaping is coming along, what great photo opportunities it'll afford—a sensible segue if Jeremy is handy."

"You talk about how excited you are to see the whole place come together, the amenities, the gleaming glass, the perfect tables and chairs," Lana picked up the line of thought.

"And how excited you are for the big opening gala we're going to hold and invite all of the press to, because this conference-slash-reception center—the whole hotel—is something special," Rosemary finished.

Cami growled. "Fine. Fine. I'll see what Vince thinks and we can give it a try. I'm not making any promises."

Jonquil's mouth split into a smile. "They won't know what hit them."

The doorbell rang and Cami saw Vince through the patio door window.

"Perfect," Lana said. "The man of the hour." She smirked at Cami. "Now you can't weasel out of asking him."

Cami glared at Lana as she moved to answer the door. Tittering came from several of the other women, which she chose to ignore. She had a moment to debate the best way to bring up the issue with Vince as she crossed the room. When Rosemary laughed at something Jonquil had whispered, Cami knew what she was *not* going to do—she was not bringing him into the house so everyone could embarrass her. When she opened the door, she smiled. "Hey, there." She nudged him so she could join him on the patio, shutting the door firmly behind her.

He took her hand. "I stopped to see if you in the fifteen minutes I had before my meeting tonight, but it looks like you're in the middle of something."

She led him to the railing and leaned against it. "There was a bad article in the paper that's cost us some bookings. We've been discussing strategy." She pursed her lips, then took the plunge. "We were just talking about how you could help, if you're willing."

He slid his hands onto her waist and moved in close. "I'm game. What do you need?"

She wrapped her arms around his neck, enjoying the light scent of his cologne, the softness of his hair under her fingers. She filled him in on the wedding furor and the plan the others had hatched. She thought she was being very casual about the whole thing, so she was surprised by his response.

He stroked his hands up her back, then down to her waist again. "Now why did telling me make you nervous? Did you think I'd refuse?" He pulled her closer, holding her gaze.

The breath sucked out of her lungs when she saw the glint in his eyes. "I guess I'm not very good at asking people for help."

"So you don't expect your sisters to step up and help solve the problem?"

"That's different. It's their job." She didn't know how to deal with this man who wanted to be there for her through everything. Trent would have milked the favor for payback many times over.

Vince leaned in, his lips a scant inch from hers, his breath feathering across her skin. "And I thought such a slight favor was my job, since you're my woman."

Normally such a possessive comment would have raised her independent hackles, but coming from him, it didn't. Their lips met in a soft caress and her brain went spinning. "Am I?"

"Most definitely." Then his mouth took hers. His hands skimmed up her back, drawing her to him. She reveled in his taut chest muscles beneath her hand and the feel of his support surrounding her.

Much too soon, he eased back. "As much as I'd like to spend the next two weeks or so kissing you, I need to grab lunch and get back to work, and you should get back to your meeting."

"Right. I better go." She slid her arms from around his neck, still light-headed, and more than a little embarrassed that they'd been kissing in full view of everyone on the other side of the windows.

"Dinner tomorrow?" he asked, nibbling on her lip.

"Yeah, well, I'll let you know. We should be done by dinnertime."

"I'll shoot for six-thirty. That'll give me time to go home and clean up. Maybe we can plan another time to hang out with your sisters."

That got her attention. "Wait," she set a hand on his chest, easing him back so she could see his eyes. "Why?" His request to spend time with everyone threw her. Sure, he'd been around them all before, but this felt too official or something. How would he fit into her unreliable family dynamic when so much was up in the air?

He tipped his face toward hers. "They're your family and they're important to you. I want to get to know them better."

She wasn't sure how she felt about most of them, so their importance was debatable, but she decided not to argue. "If you want to, we'll have to set something up."

"Great." He pressed one last, firm kiss to her lips, then pulled away, heading for his truck. "I'll see you at six-thirty."

Thrown off balance by his dismissal, she crossed the patio

and almost blindly reached for the door knob. The tabby Sage had adopted walked between her legs and pawed at the door. She nudged him aside, sucked in a steadying breath and slid through the opening.

She found everyone loading their plates with the sandwiches.

Rosemary cocked an eyebrow. "Whoa, serious lip-lock. I hope you got a yes out of him."

Cami felt herself blush as Jonquil piped up. "Totally hot. You should have invited him to join us for dinner."

Putting a hand to her hair, Cami tried to adjust to the teasing—something she and Lana rarely did with each other, and which she never did with others. It had a distinct sibling feel to it which both intrigued her, and made her nervous. "I didn't realize you were all eating or I would have brought him in."

Or not, since she wasn't ready to expose Vince to these teasing women too often—because even those who kept their thoughts to themselves gave her amused looks. She walked to Blake's side and grabbed a sandwich bun. "He wants to do a dinner thing another time, casual like, so you can meet some more people and he can get to know you all better."

"Am I invited?" Blake asked as he passed her the mustard and shuffled the mayo toward Lana.

"Of course, if you're in town."

"Great. Give me some notice and I'll arrange it." He glanced at Lana and slid the American cheese slices to her, then grabbed the Sun Chips and set them nearby.

Lana's eyes flew to him, confusion and surprise filling them before reverting back to her plate. "Thanks."

"You're welcome."

Cami narrowed her gaze at Blake as he strolled across the room, returning to his seat. There were two kinds of cheese, and three of chips, but Blake had known—without prodding—which Lana preferred. This definitely bore further scrutiny.

CHAPTER 26

The sun was high and hot when Vince saw Blake strolling in his direction the next afternoon. A man with a mission, even if he did glance around the hotel grounds, as if taking casual perusal of the beds. Vince was cleaning away the last of the weeds on the west side flower beds and double checking the sprinklers and the mowing job his guys had done. "Howdy. Finally finish your meeting?"

"Yes. This has been an unusual situation. I don't understand why someone's picking on the girls; add to that this ghost nonsense." Blake slid his hands into the pockets of his dress pants and rocked back on his heels.

"It makes me mad. Those women are doing their best, and from what I've seen so far, their best is impressive. Why would someone want to ruin it?"

"I don't know, but I'm working on it." Blake glanced at the snapdragons near his feet, and when he spoke, his tone changed. "You've been busy this summer." When his eyes shot back to Vince, it was clear he wasn't talking about landscaping.

Though it put his back up to have his motives questioned, Vince covered with a shrug. "You seem rather interested."

"It's natural."

"Because you've got a thing for Lana, or because they're your employees, more or less?" Vince wiped his hands on his pants, not worrying about dirt streaks. They were already beyond help of anything but a washing machine.

Blake's gaze was steady on him. "Because I care. And because their father asked me to watch out for them."

Vince lifted his brows. It was a very nice answer, but he thought it was only half accurate. "You have nothing to worry about, as I don't want to see any of them hurt. Least of all Cami." He hooked his thumbs in his pockets, hoping he wasn't projecting the irritation he felt at Blake's third degree and decided to turn some of it around. "And if I asked you about your intentions towards Lana?"

Blake's eyes flashed and his face hardened, his voice growing cold. "What's between Lana and I stays between us. I'm not going to hurt her and neither is anyone else."

Vince figured he was supposed to be scared, but it didn't come close. The response definitely intrigued him, though. "I feel the same responsibility to watch out for them that you do. So we understand each other."

Blake studied Vince for a long moment. "Perfectly." He put out his hand, offering it to Vince, who grinned and accepted it.

"So," Vince said as he grabbed a shovel, glad to have it over. "Did George make it clear he picked you out to be a son-in-law too?"

A slow smile crossed Blake's face. "Something like that."

"You play poker?"

"Not well."

"All the better," Vince flashed him a grin. "Though we

169

don't exactly play high stakes. Let me know when you're going to be around some Thursday, and you can join Gage, Jeremy, and me. We've been looking for a fourth since a friend of ours moved."

"I think I'd like that."

Cami burst into the house, trembling with excitement. "Mrs. Grady," she called out. The woman's car was parked out front, so Cami knew she was here. She clutched the printout as she hurried through the house, finally finding Mrs. Grady in Delphi's bedroom, washing the window.

"What is it?" Mrs. Grady turned to Cami.

Cami waved the paper in her hands. "I think I've found you some hope. A little, anyway. I just spoke with a friend of a friend in Chicago. They're working on this new database of people willing to do live organ donation. He said he could get your husband's information in the database. All he needs to do is sign the HIPAA waiver and request the relevant records be sent over. It's not a sure thing, but maybe."

Tears welled up in Mrs. Grady's eyes and she sat heavily in the gray office chair at the desk. "Are you serious?"

"It's still a small database, totally run by volunteers, but it's growing all the time. If your husband is a match, the donor will be contacted to verify that they're still willing, then there will be testing and whatever—I'm sure you're familiar with the process."

"Yes." The woman sobbed and covered her face with her hands. "I can't believe you did this."

"I haven't done much of anything yet. It was only a couple of calls." Cami had sent out a dozen emails and made two or three times that many calls, but it had been fun to have a good challenge. Managing the impossible had been her favorite part of being a concierge.

"Still, I can't believe you did this." Mrs. Grady looked up at her with wet eyes. "Why would you? I barely know you."

"Do I have to know you well to want to help? You've been so good to us. You deserve to have your husband around for a long, long time." Cami gave the woman's arm a squeeze.

Sobs tore out again and Mrs. Grady stood, moving toward the door. "Do you mind? I need to . . ."

"That's fine." Cami laughed, never happier than she was right now. "You take care of the paperwork. We'll see you tomorrow. "

Before she headed back to the office, Cami double-checked the locks, then practically danced out to her car.

Cami was ready when Vince arrived to pick her up that evening. She had no idea what he had in mind, so she'd worn stone colored dress pants, a dark red blouse with capped sleeves, and a pair of loafers, dressing it all up with some gaudy costume jewelry she'd bought two years earlier and never had the guts to wear.

Vince wore his usual T-shirt and jeans and his hair was still slightly damp. He brought her a small bouquet of pink Peruvian lilies. "Do you like them?" he asked when she accepted the flowers.

"They're perfect. Thanks." She brushed a kiss across his lips, then turned to the kitchen to find a vase.

"That's all the thanks I get?" he asked, stepping in behind her and reaching over her head to grab the vase, which was a bit too high up for her to reach comfortably.

171

"Well, I might be able to do better," she teased as she turned into his arms.

"That's what I thought." He tipped his head as he sampled her lips. "Take care of those so we can go."

She slid out of his reach, her heart pounding a lot faster than normal, as she found the kitchen shears and snipped at the stems, resettling them in fresh water. "They are beautiful. Delicate, classy, but simple."

He reached out, snagged a lock of her hair and gave it a light tug. "I hadn't planned on flowers, but they reminded me of you."

She didn't know what to do with him when he was like this. She'd had other boyfriends say sweet things, but usually the comments were too planned, maybe even on the insincere side. Not Vince, though. When she saw the look in his eyes, she believed his words.

"Done?" he asked, taking her hand.

"Yes." She followed him to the door, picking up her purse on their way out. The kitchen and great room were miraculously empty as they passed through. "So where are we going?"

He didn't answer right away, taking her around the nose of his car and settling her inside. "My place."

Vince shut the door and circled to his side without giving her a chance to respond. After the long day he'd had at work, they were going to his place? Maybe he planned to get take out.

When he pulled onto the street, she asked, "Your place? Are we stopping for burgers along the way?"

He grinned. "I am capable of cooking. Sometimes. I thought it might make a nice change. A little spaghetti, some puppy love, and uninterrupted time together."

"Sounds nice." And it did. When he reached for her hand, she threaded their fingers together, sat back, and enjoyed the ride as Jason Aldean crooned a country ballad.

The drive to his place was peppered with conversation about the day. When they pulled in front of a huge log cabin that stood two stories with a big bank of windows and a wrap-around porch, Cami thought the man had great taste in homes. She'd been too preoccupied to notice the first time she'd been there. "This is lovely."

The home was snuggled into the woods, but with a little grass for a yard, and swaths of native bushes and flowers. She could tell he'd made an effort to ensure the landscaping blended with nature. "It's like it grew there."

He grinned at her and stole a kiss before releasing her hand to exit the car. "I'm glad you approve."

How could she not, she wondered as she waited for him to get her door. Most of the homes she'd seen had either ruthlessly cut back the forest to impose out-of-place landscaping, or had let their yards grow wild. This was a perfect fusion of the two schools of thought.

After helping her out of the car, Vince reached into the back for a bag of groceries. "I stopped at the store for supplies before picking you up."

The dogs went crazy in the backyard, barking like they were under attack and jumping so their doggie noses appeared over the top of the fence for a blink. Cami looked forward to seeing them again.

The inside was as bright as outside, all clean, clear-varnished pine on walls and floors. The furniture was minimal, but cozy with warm fabrics and soft cushions. It wasn't so overtly masculine a woman would be uncomfortable, but held Vince's taste through everything.

"Look around if you'd like. You didn't last time. I'll go start dinner," Vince said.

Though a thought niggled that she ought to help, she decided to take him up on the offer to explore first. "All right. I'll join you in a few minutes."

The rest of the house fit the same mold. It could use a woman's touch: a bowl of flowers here or there, something hanging on the walls that wasn't wrought iron, or made of animal antlers—though there were no actual heads mounted, for which she was grateful.

Everything was clutter free, put where it belonged—but she supposed he probably wouldn't have invited her over if it had been a mess. When she stopped at his bedroom door, she noticed the balcony on the other side. She crossed to step out, look over the backyard, and saw him loving on the dogs. She couldn't hear what he said to them, but his voice was playful.

"Are you harassing those dogs again?" she called down to him.

He turned to see her on the balcony and grinned. Their eyes caught as the smile slid from his face. For a long moment time seemed to stop as the air backed out of Cami's lungs and something moved in her chest. Needing a chance to center herself, she waved and walked back into the house, rubbing her chest at the sudden ache. What had that been all about? Cami had never felt anything like it. She checked out the last two rooms upstairs, both of which held boxes, but no furniture, then felt centered enough to speak with him again.

She found Vince in the kitchen, standing over a pan of hamburger browning with chunks of onion in it. "Your place is nice. Clean—way cleaner than I expected." She tried to keep her voice light as she walked over. Michael Bublé's voice crooned from speakers tucked into the room corners, surprising her yet again.

"Thanks. I'm not much for clutter. Would you slice some mushrooms for the sauce?"

"Sure." Grateful to have something to do with her hands, she picked up the knife from the marble-topped island and went to work. The theme of the kitchen, like the rest of the house, was *space*. There was ample room between cabinets—and plenty of those to go around. A dining area between the kitchen and back patio held an undersized table and chairs for the space, and the back wall was almost all windows, bringing the fenced yard into the house. "This must be a spectacular place to sit in the winter."

"It is. And the fall when the leaves are all turning gold and red. And in the spring when the first hint of green becomes a haze across the mountain."

"So, pretty much year round," she said.

He chuckled. "Yeah, pretty much."

She sliced green peppers for the sauce and the salad, more mushrooms, some pretty tomatoes, which were obviously locally grown, and tossed them all into a bowl after dumping a package of field greens into it.

"I didn't picture you cooking much," Cami said when the salad was done and Vince slid garlic bread into the oven.

"You have a lot to learn about me." Vince glanced over his shoulder at her and grinned. "Okay, time to fess up. This is my best dish, by far. I eat a lot of fast food, TV dinners and cereal."

"And yet you built a kitchen like this one. Rosemary would go crazy seeing it go to waste."

"You tell her she's welcome to cook in it anytime she

wants, if it bothers her so much." He looked over at Cami after setting the timer. "Or you can come use it sometime." He slid his hands onto her waist and pulled her close. "I like seeing you here."

Cami melted a little more as Vince kissed her, soft and gentle. He released her to check on the pasta.

When they were seated at the table, twirling spaghetti on their forks Vince finished talking about one of his high school exploits. "Let's just say my mom was less than pleased. I was doing extra chores for a month."

"You deserved it." Cami looked down at her plate. "My mom definitely would've had a fit." She felt a lump of pain rise to her throat when she thought of her mom, so vibrant and young. "She was also really good at creative punishments."

Vince's hand slid over hers. "Your father said she died several years back, but he didn't say how."

Cami flipped her hand over and entwined their fingers. She rarely talked about it, but after everything they'd been through, she felt safe telling him. "Six years ago she started to act odd. She developed memory loss and dementia almost overnight. At first we wondered if it was a brain tumor or something. Then the doctor diagnosed it as Creuzfeldt-Jakob Disease."

Vince ran his thumb over her knuckles, his full attention on her. "What's that?"

"It's a neurological disorder that causes holes in the brain, makes it like a sponge. Her whole personality changed in a matter of weeks. Dad cancelled everything he was doing, passed along his work to someone else and stayed home with her." Her eyes stung with the memories she usually tried to ignore. She much preferred to think of her mother as healthy and vibrantly alive. "It was all so fast. One day she was normal, and practically overnight Dad had to hire a full-time nurse."

"How long did it take?" Vince asked.

"To kill her? Less than four months."

"Fast, too fast," he said, giving her hand a squeeze. "And agonizingly slow all at the same time."

"Yeah. It was awful." The ache in her chest grew. "I miss her every day."

A moment of silence passed between them, then he leaned in and brushed his lips against her temple. The gentleness of his touch reassured her and she leaned against him.

After dinner they played with the dogs, then enjoyed the cannoli he'd picked up at a restaurant in town.

When the dishes were all piled in the dishwasher or drying on the counter, Vince pulled her into his arms and twirled her around the room, making her laugh. "I have the sudden desire for a dance." He slid into rhythm with the music. "You don't mind, do you?"

She snuggled closer to him and inhaled his cologne. "Definitely not."

The music transitioned into "You Are Always on my Mind," dripping with smooth sounds and light piano. Vince slowed things down, pulling her closer, one hand on the small of her back, the other tangled in the curls at her nape as he nuzzled her neck, her ear, her jaw and took her mouth in a lazy, sensual kiss.

"Did someone tell you about my thing for Michael Bublé?" she asked against his lips.

177

"Hmmm? No. But I can change the music if he's competition for me."

She giggled and his hand on her back skimmed up her spine, dragging her closer as she wrapped her arms around him, kissing back with focused, languid attention. The song was long over, had moved onto another when he pulled back and kissed her again. He slid both hands on her face, taking the kiss deeper.

When he tipped his forehead against hers, she thought her heart would pound right out of her chest.

"Stay the night." His words were low, throaty, but vibrated right through her.

"I—" She shouldn't, it was a mistake, but she couldn't think clearly.

"Come on, baby. Stay with me." Vince gave her another long kiss, then slid his lips down to nibble at her neck.

"Okay." And as he led her upstairs to his room, Cami refused to let herself second-guess.

CHAPTER 27

Vince woke Cami with kisses, enjoying the way her face went from asleep to half awake, to fully aware.

"Mmm. Is it morning already?" Her voice was soft and sleepy.

"Yes, and as nice as it might be to stay here with you all day, I have to get out on a job site. I have the sneaking suspicion you have work to do as well. Sorry. Bad planning on my part."

"That's fine." She stood and stretched, wearing only the long T-shirt he'd offered her when she'd shivered in bed beside him. Vince loved her tousled curls, the pink color in her cheeks from waking warm and pliant under his kisses. He wished he could have lain in bed with her for hours longer, holding her as she slept.

He had already showered and dressed, so he pointed her toward the bathroom. "Go ahead and shower while I scramble some eggs."

"All right. I'll be fast."

"I bet." He pressed one more kiss to her lips before dragging himself away.

He'd had his share of relationships, but had never been

179

with anyone who fit so well in his life. She was strong and flexible, determined and fragile all at once. A conundrum he didn't think he'd be able to unravel anytime soon. He looked forward to trying.

As he scrambled the eggs and poured them into the hot butter, he wondered how soon he could get her back here again, in his house, in his bed. He hadn't planned for her to stay the night, but when he'd seen her on his balcony, everything just clicked inside him. Vince had thought George was crazy trying to hook him up with his rubs-elbows-with-the-elite daughter, but now he couldn't imagine anyone fitting him better. She was the one.

The question was how to get her to see things the same way.

When she came back downstairs, fully dressed, he was setting the table with juice and bacon on the side.

"It looks great," she said. "I could smell the bacon. Do you have any coffee?"

"I don't have a fancy machine, but it's hot." He gestured to the coffeemaker. "There are cups above it."

She reached into the cupboard and pulled out two. "You want a cup?"

"Yeah, thanks."

He thought it should have been awkward, the morning after, but it wasn't. They slid into sync, had a nice chat over breakfast discussing the day's plans. He dropped her back at her place with a lingering kiss, and a promise to call her later.

Cami tried to sneak into the house before realizing she should have known better. Rosemary and Jonquil sat over their espresso at the table. Both eyed her with identical grins as she entered.

"Well, well. Someone's date went better than planned," Rosemary said over her coffee cup.

"I'd have something fairly uncomplimentary to say to you about that, but I'm feeling too smug right now." Cami moved to the espresso machine and dispensed a dose for herself. The coffee at Vince's had been good, but she needed something stronger to jump-start her day.

Rosemary's response was pithy, but had no heat in it. She ended it with an innuendo-filled, "Sooo?"

Cami caught her gaze, held it, coolly. "So, what?"

"Don't give me your princess-to-peon-routine—though I must admit you do it well. Spill. I want details."

"Forget it." Cami moved toward the stairs with her espresso. She had to do something with her hair before it dried all the way. "You'll have to use your imagination." Then she couldn't help herself. "And know it was way better than that."

Jonquil laughed while Rosemary groaned.

Cami still felt smug as she closed her bedroom door behind her.

"There's something you should know about our games before we get inside," Vince said to Blake as they pulled in front of Gage's place a few nights later.

"Yeah? You play in your underwear or something?"

Vince chuckled. "No, and don't put that picture in my head. Actually, we have a long-standing tradition from when we first started playing poker at age six that we never changed. We play for pennies."

"Pennies?" The revelation made Blake blink.

Vince got out of the car and waited for Blake to join him. "Pennies. We use chips, because it feels like we're actually betting something, but we each ante up ten bucks worth of chips, play until we decide we're done for the night, then cash out." He enjoyed the disbelief as it came over Blake's face. "Last time I walked out with almost seven extra bucks in my pocket."

"Because it's really all about having a guy's night and strategy," Blake said facetiously.

"You got it." Vince slapped Blake on the back and led him into Gage's palatial Swiss-style home, calling out, "Hey, the party's here." Across the room there was a round table set up with chairs, snacks, and stacks of colored poker chips. When they joined Gage in the dining room, Vince turned to Blake. "Welcome to the future sons-in-law club."

Gage gave him a hand signal. "Oh, hell no, don't even get started."

"The future sons-in-law?" Blake asked.

"DiCarlo handpicked each of us to marry one of his girls. He was very forward thinking." Vince set the case of beer on the table.

"I don't care what he thought. No way am I giving up my freedom to marry that ice queen Delphi," Jeremy said as he brought in a bag of chips and a bottle of dip.

"Maybe if you hadn't all but opened your first conversation with 'by the way, I have no interest in marrying you,' she wouldn't treat you like the idiot you are," Vince said.

"Says the man who's gone gaga over DiCarlo daughter

number one," Gage added. "And I don't care how wonderful you say Jonquil is, I'm not giving in to any dead guy's fantasies."

Blake's lips twitched, as if holding back a laugh. "All three of you are on the docket?"

Gage shot Vince a glare. "I thought you said it was a club secret."

Vince pointed a thumb in Blake's direction. "You're looking at the fourth member of the club. Lana in his case, though he doesn't seem too reluctant."

Blake grabbed a bottle of beer, popped off the top, and took a few swallows. "There's something about a red-head."

"Dude, I can't believe you're bending to the old man." Gage sat at the table and started counting out chips.

"I actually made the choice first." Blake tipped his head. "At least I *think* I did. If not, he was way more subtle with me than he must have been with you all."

"Don't know why he'd want a ski bum marrying one of his daughters anyway," Gage said with a grin.

"Or an itinerant photographer." Jeremy slung his leather jacket over the back of the chair, sitting with them.

Vince shook his head. "That article still burns me."

"They're nice girls. They didn't deserve that," Gage agreed.

"And you did?" Blake asked.

"We're a bunch of bums, what can we say?" Gage grinned and pulled the deck of cards out of its box.

"I suppose it'll all come out when your wedding announcements hit the papers," Blake said, a smug grin on his face.

Jeremy's response was short and pithy.

"Three successful business men; Vince and Jeremy each running their own, Gage running your shared interest. It's going to be pretty," Blake said as he took a free chair.

Gage's eyes narrowed on Blake, who appeared to enjoy the response. "I manage the resort for a corporation."

"Which you three own, though admittedly, you personally own the lion's share." Blake took a potato chip from an open bag on the table.

"Where did you get that crap?" Vince asked. He didn't want the fact to become common knowledge. They were all happy with the way things stood.

"You don't honestly think George would talk his girls up to anyone he hadn't fully investigated, do you? Besides, he was thinking it might be nice to tie the resort in with the hotel, and when he got word back it wasn't for sale, he did some digging." Blake shrugged. "I guess after he met you he decided it was as well, and let it be."

"But we're silent partners." Jeremy pointed to himself and Vince. "It's like a token ownership."

Blake laughed as he grabbed a handful of pretzels. "The hell you are. I did some checking on my own. You're so silent you help run the mountain bike events, pilot and ground crew the hot air balloons, and step in working the lifts or on the maintenance when Gage gets in a bind. *Very* hands off."

Gage laughed. "He's got you there. But I'm still not interested in Jonquil."

Jeremy grabbed a manila envelope that sat on an end table, opening it on his way back. He sorted through the pictures and tossed one of Jonquil in front of Gage. "I wouldn't dismiss her if I were you."

Gage picked up the photo, his eyes nearly bugging.

"That's her? Damn, she's hot." He stared for a few more seconds, sucked in a breath, and shook his head. "Too bad I'm a confirmed bachelor. Put it away, let's start playing. No talk about any women who are actually in the realm of possibility tonight. Strictly dream girls."

Jeremy put the pictures back in the envelope, and set it on the end table again. "Those are for you to take, Blake."

"Then Delphi is totally fair game for discussion," Vince jumped on Gage's comment. "No matter what Jeremy did now, I seriously doubt he could convince her he wasn't the biggest creep on the planet,"

"Your reverse psychology isn't going to work on me. Not interested." Jeremy picked up the cards as they were dealt.

"And I wouldn't bet on Blake's chances with Lana either, from what I saw the other day."

Blake's brows lifted. "What did you see?"

"Just an interesting conversation. It looked like you were about to come to blows in the parking lot. Dude, she's *not* happy with you."

"I can be tenacious. It's all a matter of biding my time." Blake let the cards lay on the table until the last one was dealt, then shuffled through them.

"So, you're determined," Gage asked, obviously mystified.

"I can be patient, but I have every intention of bringing my woman home where she belongs." Blake set two of the cards face down on the table. "Give me two."

"Better you than me." Jeremy set down one from his hand.

"Fact is," Blake said, grinning at them, "if either of those women decided to bat their eyelashes at you two, you'd be buying a ring before you knew it. I'd lay odds on it."

"You're out of your mind." Gage dealt the rest of the cards.

"I bet you each fifty bucks, if either woman decides to take an interest in you by the end of next summer, you'll fall like a house of cards."

"I'm so in," Jeremy said, tossing in couple poker chips. "On this round and your bet."

"Me too. It'll be the easiest fifty bucks I ever made," Gage agreed.

Vince thought Blake was right, but he decided this was one of those times when discretion was in his best interest. He almost hoped the girls made a move. It could be really entertaining.

Cami was worn out from unpacking boxes and sorting files. Maybe she needed a break. She grabbed a yogurt from the mini-fridge in her office and sat at her computer, wondering who else might have registered for the gala night at the hotel. Though she felt the urge to check it daily, hourly sometimes, she'd held herself back, not wanting to go crazy watching the list grow.

It had been three days though, so she wasn't being obsessive, right? Cami pulled up the records, chose the correct date, and began to scroll. Many familiar names of journalists, other hoteliers, important people within the company, and favored guests littered the lists. She flipped along until she noticed the last name Gifford. Zelda Gifford. Delphi's last name was Gifford. Cami felt her gut twist at the thought, but forced herself to think clearly.

A quick internet search was all Cami needed to learn Delphi's mom was named Zelda. Anxious, she checked and found reservations for the other sisters' mothers—except for Rosemary, a fact that left all kinds of questions running through Cami's head. But maybe Rosemary's mom hadn't made the reservation yet. Most likely.

Of course the others would want their parents to be there. She understood. Everyone deserved to have family there to support them and this was a really big deal. Cami longed for her own mother, and even for her father, despite the fact that she was still mad at him. She would have Lana and Alex there, so it wasn't as though she wouldn't have *any* family to support her, but it wouldn't be the same—and Lana would be distracted with her own responsibilities.

Cami pushed back the sadness and realized Lana needed to know as well—this was not the kind of news you sprang on someone the day everyone checked into the hotel. She stood and walked up to the executive offices on the second floor. She greeted the receptionist and walked on through. Lana was at her desk and Blake sat beside her, peering over her shoulder and pointing to something on the computer screen.

He glanced up first and concern washed over his face. "Is something wrong?"

Cami considered whether she should ask to be alone with Lana, then decided Blake was so mixed up in everything going on there was no point in excluding him now. She shut the door and walked over to an empty chair across from them, feeling numb. "Not wrong, exactly." She met Lana's gaze as the smell of ripe strawberries wafted to her from the candle warmer on the credenza. "I was checking the guest list for the gala weekend and noticed the others—their moms are coming. I don't know how I missed it before."

"The others?" Lana asked.

Slow down and try to make sense. "Delphi, Jonquil, Sage. All of their parents have reservations. I thought I should give you a heads up."

Silence filled the room for a long moment.

"Are you okay with this?" Blake finally asked. His hand came to rest on Lana's shoulder, and he gave it a squeeze as he looked between the sisters. "It must be hard for you."

Cami watched the emotions play over Lana's face. She recognized the feelings since she felt them as well. "I'll be fine. I'm just glad I noticed now instead of being surprised at the last minute."

"No problem. It's no big deal." Lana's face looked numb despite her words.

Cami stood, not sure she believed either of them were okay.

As she left the room, she turned and saw Blake pushing hair back from Lana's unhappy face, saying something to her in a voice Cami heard only as a low, comforting rumble. She wondered again at their strange relationship, but the emotions that still pumped through her made her set it aside for now.

CHAPTER 28

Evenings in the Rockies were cool, even in early August, so after double checking her form-fitting blouse, her boot-cut jeans and new cream-colored cowboy boots, Cami grabbed a summer sweater she could slide on later.

Cami met Vince at the bottom of the stairs, her heart pattering with excitement as he watched her descend.

"Wow. Have I said that enough lately?" He pulled her in, pressing a languid kiss to her lips.

"I don't think you could ever overuse that word," she murmured when they came up for air.

"Yes, he could," Rosemary said from where she sat at the dining table. "But of course, he's completely right. Those jeans were made for you."

"And the jewelry is awesome," Jonquil added.

"I guess I pass inspection." Amused, Cami looped her arm through Vince's and allowed him to lead her to the door. "Have a good night," she called over her shoulder.

"Not as good as you, I'm thinking," Rosemary shot back.

Cami felt her face heat.

"You get caught coming in the other morning?" Vince asked when they were in the open air.

"Oh, yeah."

He helped her into the car, then joined her and pulled into the street. He talked about work, but she could barely listen, thinking about the party ahead with little idea of what to expect. Her hatred of big parties, especially ones filled with strangers, filled her chest with anxiety, nudging at her usual core of confidence. She hoped she didn't become too

189

nauseated to eat—a problem she often dealt with at large social gatherings.

"What's wrong?"

She smiled weakly. "I'm a little nervous."

"Hon, I have a feeling this is going to be nothing like the parties you're used to." His hand covered hers in her lap and gave it a squeeze. "No need to worry. It'll be fine."

Time to deflect the comment before he realized how much her stomach churned. "If it were going to be like my other parties, I sure wouldn't be wearing these boots." She admired them again, liking them, despite their being so different from her usual footwear.

"I like those boots. And Rosemary's completely right about the jeans."

She laughed in pleased embarrassment.

"I'm glad you're coming with me tonight," he said, twining his fingers through hers.

"I enjoy being with you." She shrugged, feeling awkward. "Besides, it's my job."

"It's more than a job; it's family pride and love of what you accomplish." He squeezed her hand.

He understood. Tingles of emotion rolled through her. She didn't think he would grasp the way she felt about it. "That too."

Vince lifted her hand, pressing it to his lips. "You're an amazing woman, Cami."

"Tell me again when we convince the happy couple they want to keep their wedding at the resort."

He smiled against her knuckles. "I've enlisted some help there. Do what you do best, and before you know it, the bride will be begging you to keep her business."

"This I gotta see."

The first hour of the party went about as Cami had imagined it. She met dozens of new people, only a fraction of whose names she recalled ten minutes later. The food was a festive mix of Jell-O salads, spicy Mexican dishes, and old favorites. Upbeat tunes spanning three decades lilted through the air and the fresh scent of pine permeated everything—but because of the upcoming discussion, Cami couldn't enjoy it. Vince knew everyone, asked them about their sister, son, cousin or grandmother. He talked about water shortages with the ranchers and the high school football team's chances at the state title.

He helped her make connections not only *with* the locals, but about how they related to each other. And while Cami had been used to paying attention to those kinds of things in the city, Vince did it with a relish she never felt—and out of a genuine concern for everyone around him instead of in the scheming worry about social rank that motivated so many of her acquaintances. She knew every town had its social pitfalls and expectations. She wondered, though, if he cared more about the people than she did, or if he was really good at acting sincere.

Cami suspected it was the former and was fascinated to see how enmeshed in the community he was. No wonder he had returned to Juniper Ridge after completing his degree.

His ease and familiarity and the warmth of his hand in hers eventually soothed her, lessening her anxiety.

She and the future bride greeted each other in passing, and though Cami wanted to get it over with, she knew it was too soon to bring up the wedding. These things took planning and precision and nerves of steel—at least, they did if you didn't want to be at the party. And despite everything, she would much, much rather have been cuddled with Vince on his sofa. Or wherever else he wanted to cuddle.

At dinner Vince maneuvered them so they sat with Jeremy and his date, Gage and his mother, and within hearing distance of the future bride. While everyone enjoyed the black forest cake the hostess had provided, Gage's mother, Diane, started in, "Cami, I've heard so much about your conference center. The pictures Jeremy shot are breathtaking. Seriously, every bride within fifty miles is going to want to be married there."

My cue. Cami plunged in enthusiastically, "You're so sweet, but I have to agree. Things have come together now. The last of the furniture is arriving. I love the tablecloths and vases and all of the accessories we've ordered for the room. We're using it for the grand opening gala and Delphi has kept all of the details so together. She's amazing."

Jeremy nodded reluctantly. "She's very organized, efficient. Made sure everything I needed was handy when I did pictures there."

"My niece and her boyfriend are talking about getting married. She'd love to stop by and see what you have to offer," Diane said.

Cami glanced at the bride-to-be out of the corner of her eye and saw both members of the happy couple listening in. "The sky's the limit. Sage has plans to offer wedding-morning massages for bride and groom so they can relax, along with facials or anything else they need to feel their best, and Jonquil is incredible with flowers. She's working on the most gorgeous arrangement with roses and lilies. She had so many ideas for the big party. The pastry chef Rosemary just hired is to-die-for incredible. Her cakes are like edible joy. Everything's coming together so well, I can hardly wait." She turned to Vince, smiled. "And of course the grounds are more beautiful every day."

"She wanted a fall wedding—I know, they're in a hurry and scheduling is tight. Is there any way you could fit her in?" Diane asked.

"We do have a few open weekends left, and we just had a cancellation, so everyone but Jeremy is available that day." She looked at Jeremy. "Your schedule must be pretty full."

"Yes, but Delphi can check my availability and add sessions from her office, so she should have no trouble coordinating."

"Great." She turned back to Gage's mom. "Didn't I tell you everything's falling right into line?"

"It sounds like it."

Apparently Gage had his fill of the cheesy rah-rah talk because he changed the subject. Cami was just as glad—being that perky always made her face tired. Another glance at the bride and groom, though, showed them whispering quietly and shooting looks in her direction.

CHAPTER 29

The evening's efforts were rewarded late the next morning when the bride called to reschedule her wedding, apologizing and saying they just had cold feet—as if Delphi would forget their comments about finding a different venue. Cami listened in the living room as Delphi assured the client that she could get the event reinstated, though there would be a fee to reestablish the appointments, since the vendors may have been working to fill the slot.

Delphi ended the call and danced in a circle. "Whatever you did last night, it worked. She's hooked."

"I'm not sure that's a blessing, considering what a pain she's been to work with so far, but with everything else hitting the fan, we need all the bookings we can get," Cami said.

"I don't care how difficult she is, I'm going to make this the wedding of the century, so everyone she knows will have to book here too."

"Don't crow too long and loud," Blake said as he entered through the front door, Jonquil trailing behind him. "The report about the prince cancelling his reservation hit the news this morning, and we've already had several more cancelations."

Cami swore but stopped when he held up a hand.

194

"There's more. A story got out about your father calling to talk to each of you at least twice a week, and making clandestine visits to your homes every-other month. I don't know how much is true—"

A cold prickle slid down her spine and Cami stood and hollered at the top of her lungs, "Emergency meeting now! Everyone get your butts in here."

Women came upstairs and downstairs and with a little calling back and forth, everyone was in the room within a minute. Cami stood and faced the other women, studying each of their faces as they arrived in the room. "Did anyone discuss your visitation schedules and phone calls with Dad outside this room?" When everyone just stared at her, she explained, "There's an article in the paper about it, so if any of you shared it with other people, we need to know who so we can figure out where our leak is."

Everyone looked around them while murmurs of "not me" and "I didn't" filled the room.

"You think we've been bugged?" Lana asked.

Cami looked at Blake. "We discussed the visits and phone calls in this room. If it got to the press, we need to get someone in here to sweep for bugs like yesterday."

Blake pulled out his cell phone and dialed. After he finished a quick conversation, he turned back to them. "Joel will be here with the right equipment within the hour. Is there any other sensitive information you've discussed in here?" He looked around. "Then again, maybe we should take this outside."

Everyone agreed and they moved to the lawn, far from the porch railing.

Cami tried to think of everything they'd said in their

conversation the previous week, her heart sinking. "We discussed my relationship with Vince. General plans for the hotels. Specifics about applicants. Way too much that shouldn't become public knowledge. And if they have a bug in the great room, who's to say there isn't one in other rooms as well? Or cameras?"

"Oh no. What if someone recorded me trying to do Zumba?" Delphi looked horrified.

"Har, har. You think this is funny?" Lana asked, crossing her arms over her chest.

Delphi glared at Lana. "No, I don't think this is funny—an elephant is more graceful than I am."

"Not true," Rosemary piped up. "You're somewhat more graceful than an elephant. At least equal to a rhino."

"Thanks." Delphi shot her a nasty glare. "Maybe you set up the bugs. You don't seem to care who knows about your life. You're so open with no secrets to hide."

Rosemary's jaw dropped, then she narrowed her eyes. "I can't believe you would say that. I have as much to lose as you do."

"Right. You, who claim you could get a job anywhere so you don't need your inheritance."

"I don't. And I'm not the one who stormed out in the middle of the reading of the will."

"Enough." Blake raised his voice so it covered the two women. "Give it a rest. None of you have anything to gain by bringing the group down. It just comes out of your pocketbook if the hotel loses money and you're all under the microscope."

"There haven't been any bad articles with her name headlining," Rosemary pointed out.

"In some social circles, the fact that I'm known to be related to you is enough."

"Seriously, you two," Lana said. "Drop it. Joel will find out what's going on."

Cami hoped Lana was right.

"For now, maybe we ought to assume someone is listening to everything you say, and take any sensitive conversations to the office," Blake said.

"Right. We have new employees to train today and we need to get moving," Lana said, standing up. They were already going to be late.

"I'll stay and let Joel in, then meet you all at the hotel," Sage offered.

"Good idea. I'll send you all a text when he's done here and we'll coordinate a meeting in Lana's office—if that's okay with you?" Blake asked, though it was clear the question was mostly a matter of form.

Lana pressed her lips together and nodded, whether she felt he was overstepping, or she was upset by current events, it was impossible to tell. "I'm leaving in five minutes if any of you want to ride with me." She headed back inside.

Cami followed, gathered her things and slid them into the attaché she'd been using. She needed at least ten minutes for makeup before she'd be ready. It was going to be a long day.

∞≫

Staff meeting had to wait until 4:30 when everyone had sent home the new hires for the day. They met in Lana's office, all crowded into the tight space, and waited for Joel. When he entered, his face was grim.

"If you want to give us your report, we'll go from there," Lana said as the door shut behind him.

"We found four cameras that aren't part of the main system, and a dozen bugs. I believe we've cleaned everything out, and there are a few partial prints on the bugs. The sheriff is running them now against a list Sage gave me of everyone she could think of who had access to the house. In the meantime, I've had all the locks and codes changed. We found a recording device on site which was grabbing the signals for download. Then it would transmit the information to someone outside the house, probably in a car on the road."

He glanced around the room, his normally serious face more severe than usual. "So the good news is the person responsible probably isn't in the house often, but the perpetrator did have to gain access to put in the bugs and cameras. Is there any time you can think of when the house hasn't been locked up tight?"

Cami shook her head and noticed the others doing so. "Sage is completely paranoid about setting the alarm and double checking every door and window lock at night and before we leave the place empty—even when we're there most of the time."

"As she should be. As you *all* should be. Your safety isn't a joke." He sent Sage an approving nod. Joel produced a bunch of keys and passed them around. "These fit the new locks." He told them the new pass code for the garage and the house. "I'll be over tonight and we'll reset the garage door openers as well for each of your cars. Until then, make sure to keep the door between the garage and the house locked at all times. Actually, that's not a bad precaution to take in any case. I'll be hanging around a lot for the next few days, monitoring the system to see if we can catch the person downloading the data."

Cami felt her stomach twist. She'd thought their current security efforts had been pretty strict, but this was going to make her crazy. "Do you think we're in physical danger?"

His eyes strayed to Sage. "It's impossible to know. So far they've been focused on discrediting you, but it's always best to be careful. I also don't want any of you walking out to your cars here or at the hotel unless there's someone with you, either one of your sisters or one of my security team. Not until we straighten this out."

Cami reminded herself these were precautions designed to prevent problems, not because of an immediate threat. But because of what Joel found at the house, it felt like a threat. She hated thinking she couldn't trust anyone around her.

When she walked out of the meeting a while later, Vince waited in the hallway.

She felt a rush of pleasure at seeing him. "What are you doing here?"

"Blake called. He said I should be here when your meeting ended." He pulled her under his shoulder and kissed her softly. "What's going on?"

Cami caught Blake's eye and mouthed a thank you to him. He smiled and turned his attention back to Lana. Cami sighed and met Vince's brown eyes. "Can I come over to your place?"

A smile spread. "Of course. Let's swing by the house and grab some of your stuff. You can stay the night."

It sounded wonderful.

Since Cami had ridden to the hotel with Sage, she let Vince drive her home, and explained what was going on as they went. At her place she packed a quick bag and left her car keys with Jonquil so the garage door opener could be reset. "I'm going." She held up the bag in explanation, not wanting to say too much aloud, though Joel said the bugs were all gone.

"See you tomorrow?" It would be Saturday, so they were pretty much taking a break for the weekend, though she had work to deal with on her laptop.

Vince slid an arm around Cami's back, leading her to the door. "Monday morning."

Jonquil winked before they headed out.

When they'd left her house, Cami hadn't been certain about staying at Vince's through Monday morning—it seemed like a huge step. They had a great time together though, sitting out on the patio, taking a long ramble in the woods with the dogs, and making more meals than had been prepared in the kitchen in a month's time before. And when they made love, she was amazed the magic hadn't been her imagination or a one-time thing.

Monday morning Vince dropped her back at her home instead of work because she hadn't brought an appropriate work suit.

He kissed her just inside the doorway, taking his time with it. "Maybe you should move in with me," he suggested.

"Can't. Contract says I have to live in this house." She wasn't sure if she was relieved or disappointed about that stipulation with his tempting alternative. The weekend had been an idyll of sorts, not real life, and she knew moving in would change everything.

He groaned as she pulled away. "Don't tell me I have to wait until next September."

"Unless you want to marry her, that's the deal." Jonquil headed up the nearby stairs.

Cami could have sworn they had been talking too low for anyone to hear them, but apparently the baby of the group had ears like a dog.

"Oh, is that all?" Vince grabbed Cami's chin and turned her face back, kissing her again.

"All?" Cami asked when she was allowed to talk again. "Isn't it more than enough?"

"Plenty. I'm more than happy to get married. What do you say?" he asked between pressing kisses to her mouth and cheeks and chin.

"Whoa." She pushed him away, ran those words back through her head to make sure she'd heard right. "You're out of your mind. We've only been dating a few weeks."

"Six, but who's counting? And sometimes six years isn't long enough to decide if someone is the right one for you, but this time, I'd say six weeks is plenty." He leaned in for another kiss.

Though she wanted to slide back under his spell, she moved out of his reach. "You're crazy."

"About you." His slid his hands onto her waist and pulled her close.

"And unoriginal."

"But you love me anyway."

She laughed, unable to help herself as she tucked her face into his neck, loving the smell of his aftershave, though there was still a rich field of stubble he hadn't bothered to shave that morning. As for loving him, she wasn't sure if what she felt was strong enough to marry on—it was too early to make that kind of commitment. Besides, she had more pressing things on her mind. Though she'd been putting it off, she decided to address one of those issues now. "So I have this favor to ask, and you can feel free to say no if you need more notice."

"What's that?" He brushed the hair back from her face, tucking it behind her ear, teasing the sensitive lobe as his finger followed the curve.

She shivered. She'd spent a long time the previous night lying awake, considering whether or not to ask, and now her heart raced as she wondered if it was a mistake. "I have a party in Chicago Thursday night. I wondered if you'd like to go with me. I kept my condo available. I know you might have to juggle your work and getting a plane ticket can be a pain, and it's bound to cause more speculation, but—"

She stopped talking when he pressed his mouth to hers. "I'd love to go with you, Cami. Email me the flight information and I'll make a reservation."

"Okay. That's great." She nudged him away, feeling awkward though he'd made it easy—maybe *because* he'd made it easy. "Go to work. I can't think when you're kissing me."

"Good." But he pressed a quick peck to her forehead and turned away. Before he shut the door behind him, he glanced back. "I promise more finesse when I officially propose."

Cami didn't have a chance to respond before he was gone. She sucked in a breath, not sure how she felt about the fact that he was already thinking marriage.

CHAPTER 30

Joel hadn't been kidding when he said he'd be spending a lot of time at the house. Though Cami had been at Vince's for the weekend, she heard he'd hung around since dinnertime on Friday and had used Sage's bathroom to clean up and shower. He even slept on the sofa in the great room while one of his security crew monitored the machines.

She was glad to have missed most of that.

Tuesday evening most of them were sitting around the house taking care of paperwork and making plans when Joel grinned—an odd expression for his face considering how seldom he did it. "Gotcha." He pressed a few more keys, then gestured to Sage to come over and sit in his spot. "Someone just logged on to the system. I'm going to go see if I can find the person trying to download information. Stay here." He pulled a handgun from the small of his back, cocked it to load a bullet in the chamber, and put it back in the holster before heading for the door.

Cami felt her stomach drop. Joel had a gun in her house? Was that necessary? A few seconds passed as she thought about it before she realized that of course he'd be armed. This was Joel, military to the max. He probably owned an arsenal.

Maybe it should have made her feel better, safer, but somehow, it didn't.

A long moment passed and Cami started to get anxious. She inched over to the front windows, peeking out of the corner through the curtain so no one outside would be able to see her. She saw Joel just through the trees, kneeling on the ground. He looked like he had someone restrained, but she couldn't see who through the brush.

"Get away from there," Sage hissed.

"He's got someone." Cami moved to the door and opened it a crack. "Joel, do you need me to call someone?"

He looked up at her, his face grim. "Call the sheriff's office. And keep everyone inside."

"What?" She looked behind her and saw everyone else watching her. "Stay here. He's got the perp. I'll see if he need anything else. Stay inside."

No one else seemed interested in following her so Cami shut the door behind her and made her way across the grass. She pulled out her phone and dialed 911.

When she was told a deputy was on the way, she put away her phone.

"Get back inside, Cami. I don't need you out here." Joel sat between her and the person he was restraining. "If you come out, your sisters will be next. You're a distraction. Go back inside."

"Who is it?" After all of the stress and worry, she had to know who was behind everything.

"Go inside. There could be someone else out here too."

Cami studied him for a moment then shook her head. "If there were, you would have incapacitated that person and be out looking for the second person already."

204

He swore low under his breath. "Just go back inside. I'll be in as soon as I give my statement to the deputy."

There was the sound of sirens in the distance and Cami shifted, trying to see who was behind Joel.

"Go. Inside." His brows V-ed over his eyes in anger.

"Even Cami wasn't crazy enough to risk ticking Joel off. "Fine. I'll see you there."

Before she reached the front door, Rosemary opened it. "Who is it?"

"I don't know. He was hiding the guy. He insisted we stay inside."

Rosemary put her hand on her hip. "And you just turned around and came back inside like a good little girl?"

"Hey, you want to risk his wrath, that's on you, but I don't recommend it. Besides," she looked over her shoulder as the sheriff's office truck came to a stop, "Looks like he's got backup, and going over there now will just put us in their way. Better to watch out the window and see who they haul off."

"So we wuss out and let him have his way?"

"Yes. For a few minutes, anyway. Give him time to take care of things and then we can all gang up on him for answers." It galled her to have to wait when the answers were in her front yard. A second sheriff's truck pulled into the driveway. "Looks like they're planning a party out there."

"Too bad we're not invited," Rosemary said.

Delphi sat at the kitchen island while Rosemary prowled around like an agitated lion. She may have growled once or twice as well.

Cami stood at the window, watching the deputy show up, talk to the suspect and then pull out a set of handcuffs. She tapped her foot as she watched the man haul someone away.

"It's a woman." Cami couldn't believe it. She stared, trying to figure out who it was. She didn't catch any of her face, though, and the deputy pushed her in front of him, so Cami couldn't get a clear view.

"What do you mean it's a woman?" Rosemary joined her at the window, pulling back the curtains. The deputy had already pushed her into the back seat of the truck. "I missed it." She strained to get a better view of the woman until the truck pulled out, then she resumed pacing.

The second deputy stayed out talking to Joel for at least ten more minutes before taking off with a written statement. Joel headed toward the house, his mouth in a firm line.

"Here he comes." Cami twitched the curtains back in place and moved to open the door before he reached the front porch.

"You're so impatient," he said as he passed her on his way through the door.

"That's my middle name. So who was it? I couldn't tell when they hauled her off." She crossed her arms over her chest and stared him down.

He was, predictably, unfazed. He waited until everyone stood around, watching him, before he answered. "It was Mrs. Grady."

Cami felt like the breath had been knocked out of her. "No way. She would never do that to us."

Everyone else had similar reactions, filling the air with cries of disbelief and anger.

"Why would she do that to us?" Sage asked after the initial burst of questions.

"Money, of course," Delphi said, her arms crossed over her chest.

"But how could she? Does she know what she's done?" Jonquil asked. "I trusted her."

"I shared my cannoli recipe with her." Rosemary said, incredulous. "I don't share that with anyone."

Everything Cami thought she knew about the woman fell apart. Why had she hurt them even after Cami had gone out of her way to help find Mr. Grady a kidney donor?

When everyone watched him, the hubbub quiet, Joel spoke again. "Someone offered her a whole lot of money to send the records off of the security system. She claims she doesn't know who it is, but she needed the money, the medical bills were getting out of control. She apologized, for what it's worth." The disgust on his face said the apology wasn't worth much to him.

"You ought to be able to trace the money, right?" Cami asked Joel.

"I'm sure going to try." The determination in his eyes said failure was not an option.

Cami hoped with the information leak out of the way, this nightmare would come to an end.

CHAPTER 31

Though they'd seen each other again before their trip to Chicago, Vince didn't bring up the issue of marriage. Cami's thoughts seemed to zip between Mrs. Grady's betrayal and his suggestion—which had been offered as casually as if he had been proposing they take a day-trip into Denver.

If Jonquil had heard Vince's comment—Cami refused to think of it as a proposal—she hadn't said anything about it, which suited Cami fine. It was bad enough the words kept popping back up into her mind; having it turn into a discussion topic among the sisters would be way too much.

The journey was uneventful but Cami found she enjoyed having Vince with her during the flight. It was nice to have interesting conversation and laughter handy, and despite not pulling out her laptop to work as she usually did on flights, she didn't get antsy for something to do. Maybe, she thought, that was part of Vince's charm.

After they settled into Cami's condo, she checked her closet, but wasn't happy with anything in it.

"Problems?" Vince asked, coming into the bedroom fifteen minutes after she'd disappeared into the closet.

"I know I have plenty of clothes, but nothing feels quite right for the party tonight." She bit her lip, considered a demure peach dress with a flirty mid-calf skirt. "Would you mind terribly if I made a run to find something new?"

He turned her, pulling her into his arms. "Are you talking a four-hour shopping spree?"

"No way, I'll leave that for Lana. A run to Ralph Lauren for a new dress, maybe pop into Nordstrom for shoes, and home again, an hour or so max. Well, plus travel time."

He met her eyes and his lips quirked. "Will I have a chance to see you try on sexy dresses?"

She laughed. "Quite likely."

He nuzzled her neck, raising goose bumps along her side. "Perhaps I should go along to give my opinion."

"You want to go dress shopping with me?" No way was that reality. A guy like Vince didn't sit quietly by while the woman shopped. She didn't think the Y chromosome worked that way.

"Not for a full afternoon, no, but for an hour or so. And maybe while we're out, we could get some of that famous Chicago pizza I've heard about."

She grinned. "I see, it's all about the pizza."

"And seeing you in a sexy dress or three." He wiggled his eyebrows.

"How can I argue?" She pulled from his embrace and grabbed her purse. "Let's go."

Because her car was in Colorado now, they'd opted to walk, take the commuter train, or use taxis for the two-day visit. Since the station was close, they headed for the commuter train.

The run into Ralph Lauren was fairly quick and successful. She found something on the second try, a red silk sheath that ended above the knee. The neckline was more daring than her usual, but it fit her mood. She didn't model it for Vince, opting to make it a surprise.

"I can't believe you didn't show it to me. That's the only reason I came." Vince complained as they walked into Nordstrom a few minutes later.

"Hush. It'll be worth the suspense. I promise." Cami patted him on the cheek and continued on to the shoe department. There was something about shoes and Nordstrom that she could never separate.

In no time she seized a pair of Manolo Blahnik gold metallic strappy sandals with a two-inch heel to go with her new dress, then indulged herself with a Phillip Lim multi T-strap pump in black and maroon, and nearly had contortions trying to prevent herself from buying the cutest pair of Isola brown suede boots. She lost the fight, but didn't care anymore when she handed Vince the bags as they left the shop.

When Vince grumbled that she'd only brought him to be a pack animal, she smiled and gave him a quick kiss. "I'm carrying the dress."

"Which you haven't let me catch so much as a glimpse of, thank-you-very-much. And what is it with you and shoes?"

"Sorry, I can't help myself. I have a weakness for great footwear. I have just the thing for the boots, but I'll have to find an outfit to go with the pumps."

"Hold on." He stopped in the middle of the sidewalk and gave her an incredulous look. "You're going to buy an outfit to match the shoes? Isn't that backward?"

She laughed. "You'd think so, wouldn't you? But no, not in this case. Lana will completely agree with me when she sees the shoes. It's a good thing she has such tiny feet—or she might try to borrow them."

"I had no idea you were such a slave to fashion. I thought you were just naturally put together." Despite his comments, he wore a smile to match hers, and didn't appear the least put out about his shoe burden. "Now, are we going to get pizza? I'm starving."

"Almost there. You know, sometimes I think you have the appetite of a thirteen-year-old boy."

He simply grinned.

Cami grinned back, hardly able to believe she'd found someone like Vince. Two months earlier she would have sworn guys like him didn't exist—they hadn't in her world. She wasn't going to complain.

Vince's eyes popped as Cami stepped into the living room where he'd been waiting for her. He set down the soda in his hand and turned off the baseball game, giving her his full attention.

Cami gave a little spin, pleased with his expression and felt like a sexy model. "Was it worth the wait?"

"Yeah, it was." Vince walked over, taking her mouth in a long kiss. "You sure we have to go out?"

She laughed. "That was kind of the point of the trip."

"Pity." He took her hands and two stepped her around the room—it wasn't a big space, so it didn't take long. "I'd love to have you to myself all evening. But I can probably share you long enough to take care of business."

She was out of breath when they came to a stop, though very little of it was from the exertion of the dance. "That's good of you."

"I know. I'm a real catch."

She looked at his cocky grin and had to kiss him again.

211

He was a catch, the kind of man any woman would be lucky to call her own. She touched his freshly shaved cheek and pressed a chaste kiss to his mouth, a feeling of warmth building inside her every moment. This was love. Was it strong enough to last? She didn't know.

He released her and tugged on his suit coat. "Do I pass muster?" He looked incredible in a suit, making Cami think she'd better keep him close so someone else didn't try to snatch him up at the party.

"You look pretty wonderful too." She leaned in, sniffed. "And you smell terrific."

He took her hand. "Let's go wow them."

"Would you like something to drink?" Vince asked Cami when they'd been circulating for nearly an hour.

Cami smiled, already wishing the night would end. "Thanks. I'm parched. No more alcohol, though, I need to stay alert in this crowd." She watched him go, then turned to track the prince of Denmark's cousin, whom she'd seen only ten feet away a moment before. Instead, Trent moved to greet her. The low burn of nerves in her stomach grew worse. This wasn't going to be pretty.

She couldn't help but compare her ex to Vince, though she knew it was bad form. Trent's unnatural tan, bleached blonde hair, and artificially whitened teeth seemed false to her now that she'd been around a man like Vince who didn't worry about making the proper impression every moment of the day.

"Hello, Camellia, you've met Trina, haven't you?" Trent introduced the brunette on his arm.

"Of course, how are you doing, Trina? How's your

212

mother?" Cami was relieved Trent had moved on, but wondered if Trina realized what a jerk he was.

"She's well. We've both been busy getting the hospital benefit up and running. It sounds as though you've had your hands full with the hotel opening." Trina Sanders was a sweet girl with impeccable manners and a friendly attitude. Cami had always liked her. She also came from a very wealthy family, and would certainly have the cash to settle Trent's debts. Word through the grapevine was the couple had been dating since early July. More than one guest had made sure to inform Cami of that fact since her arrival at the party.

"Yes, it's been quite an undertaking, but exciting too, seeing it all come together. I know my father would have been so happy with how things are going. The party is less than three weeks away." Cami put on a smile and pretended she hadn't a care in the world about media problems.

"I know you've had some troubles. It's a shame about the Denmark royals canceling. Maybe they'll rebook after you've had time to establish yourself and prove you're capable of managing such a huge endeavor. Right now you're six untried women," Trent's words were cloying and patronizing.

Anger burned in her. "Hardly untried. We've each been working in our various departments for years, and we've found excellent employees to help carry the load. Our head of security is capable of handling any emergency, and Delphi has every angle of this release planned to the millisecond. We're going to succeed not because we're lucky, but because we're very good at what we do."

"Have you seen their work? Do you know these women will step up and do what needs to be done?" he asked. "Your father pulled them from who knows what jobs—"

It was all Cami could do to keep her voice level as the anger burned through her. "My father may have had ulterior motives for bringing us all on board with the hotel launch, but he wouldn't have risked his resort's best interest. My sisters are among the best in the business. I've seen them in action, I've seen them in difficulty and they're more than up to the task."

Miffed, Trent pushed in a different area. "And what about your lawn boy? I thought I saw him with you earlier." He smiled maliciously.

The rage cooled to ice as Cami realized he was jealous. "My *lawn boy* has a master's degree in landscape architecture from Cornell University. He's a successful businessman who employs nearly forty people, and his business is growing every year."

Vince walked up behind Cami, slid his arm around her from the right, and offered her a glass of Perier—she'd decided one glass of champagne was her limit. "Here you are, honey."

"Thanks." She flashed him a smile, grateful for the interruption. "Vince Talmadge, I'd like you to meet Trina Sanders and Trent Doyle."

The expression on Trent's face turned slightly sour as he gave Vince the once over, but Trina met him with a pleasant smile and genuine interest.

"I can see what drew you to him, Cami—intelligent *and* handsome. Always a good combination. It's good to meet you." Trina took Vince's hand in a warm shake, though not with the overt interest some of the female guests had shown. She was too classy to do that even if she had been interested.

"You flatter me," Vince said. "It's a pleasure to meet

you." His expression became speculative as he turned it on Trent, who stared at him through narrowed eyes. "And you. Have you known Cami long?"

"A while." Trent's voice was infused with innuendo, and there was an edge of mean in his eyes. "So what do you think about the run of bad publicity she and her sisters have had?"

Vince shrugged, though Cami sensed him stiffen beside her. "Someone's got a vindictive streak, but they're an amazing group of women. I wouldn't count them out—they're going to blow everyone's socks off. If you don't have other plans, perhaps you should come to the grand opening gala. See for yourself."

"I'll make our reservation in the morning. I could use some mountain air," Trina said, threading her hand around Trent's elbow. "Can you arrange to come with me?" she asked him.

"Of course, sweetheart." He put his hand over hers and smiled at her.

The thought of Trent at the hotel made Cami grit her teeth, but she forced a smile. "I'll see you there. I have a few more people I need to speak with, if you don't mind."

Trina nodded. "Of course. I'm sure you have a lot to take care of while you're in town."

Cami said her goodbyes, and she and Vince walked away.

"That was interesting," Vince muttered to her. "Is Trent an ex-boyfriend? He acted a little jealous."

"Something like that." They only made it a few steps before she spotted the prince's cousin nearby and turned Vince in his direction. "I'll explain later."

"Ah, Miss DiCarlo," the man said when he spotted her.

"I've heard so many fascinating rumors about your hotel." His eyes were warm and friendly.

"I'd hoped to speak to you about that, actually. Do you have a minute?"

He took her hand and bowed over it, kissing her knuckles. "For you, always." He introduced himself to Vince, then suggested they find a quiet corner.

"I'd love to." Cami took Vince's hand and they followed in his wake.

Vince watched Cami move around her apartment after they left the party that night. She kicked off her shoes and dug through her bags, chattering about the people they'd met.

She was like a lick of flame in her dress, sultry and eye-catching without trying. She'd worked her way through the groupings of people, chatting, kissing cheeks, laughing off reports of ridiculous rumors. Even now she was wound up from the party, not appearing the least worn down from the long evening after the cross-country flight and shopping trip.

He worked in hard, physical labor all day and he was ready to drop. How had she done it?

Cami turned to him, holding something silky with a generous helping of lace the color of champagne. "As parties go, I think it went well. Don't you agree?"

His heart twisted in his chest. She only planned on staying in Colorado for a year. She loved Chicago—she hadn't even sold her condo. "Yeah. You were amazing." How was he going to convince her to stay in Juniper Ridge when she had a vibrant social life here?

"You're no slouch yourself. And, seriously, that suit is a

killer on you." She ran one hand down his lapel, making the worry and yearning twist together in his gut.

"Not half as killer as this dress is on you." Vince was definitely curious about the bit of fabric she still held in one hand, but decided he had other priorities. He slid his hands around her waist and pulled her close. She melted into his embrace and he felt home.

CHAPTER 32

The next morning Cami and Vince walked hand in hand past a row of shops on Michigan Avenue.

"Where are we going?" he asked. "You've been mulling something over all morning."

When Cami had woken at two a.m. she'd replayed her conversation with Trent and came to a startling realization—she really did think her sisters were amazing. Well, Rosemary was seriously irritating, and Delphi stayed pretty aloof, but they were still incredible at their jobs. What was more, Cami liked the women and was starting to feel like maybe they would make the connections their father had wanted.

She gave Vince's hand a squeeze and was glad he was there to talk to. "Ever since I found out about my sisters, I've been angry and kept myself apart from them. I didn't want to get to know them, or like them. At best, I hoped we could stand to live together until the end of next August. Last night at the party, when I told Trent I would stand behind my sisters, I realized I meant it. We've pulled together, stepped up. They're funny and always teasing each other about something. I never expected to feel close to them."

His gaze caught hers and warmed her as they continued walking. "But now you do."

"Not like I feel with Lana, but we're getting there. Not only that, but after the way I've drawn back from them, I feel like I should do something—something to say yes, we're sisters, we're a unit, and of course, I thought I'd do it with jewelry." Something tangible they could all wear the day of the hotel's grand opening.

"Is someone on this street going to have six of something you can take home with you today?" He checked his watch. "We have to leave for the airport in a couple of hours."

"I thought I might have something custom made, so it's all about us. I'll ask the designer what he thinks." She caught the smile on Vince's face. "What?"

He pulled her to a store doorway, out of the rushing crowd, and turned her into his arms. "I think you're pretty great."

She wound her arms around his neck and nibbled on his chin. "I think you're pretty great, too."

He caught her mouth in a quick kiss, then moved them back into the flow of foot traffic. "So where are we going?"

She pointed to a store with a familiar logo. "Tiffany's—where else? There are lots of other stores around if you want to do some browsing of your own while I'm inside. I'll probably be an hour or so."

"I think I'll do that."

He squeezed her hand at the store entrance. "Call me if I'm not waiting inside when you finish."

She pushed open the doors, anxious to see what she and the jeweler could whip up between them.

Cami was in a great mood when Vince brought her home that evening. She walked in carrying her small bag, while Vince muscled in her big suitcase—not that it was exactly strenuous for him to carry. "Hello, everyone! I'm home!" she called as they came in the door. Vince had tried to convince her to go to his place for the night, but she'd demurred, anxious to see her sisters again after her epiphany and knowing she needed a good night's sleep before jumping back into work in the morning. He was a little too distracting sometimes.

"Only you would consider your arrival a reason for the whole house to celebrate," Rosemary said, coming around the staircase to see her. Jonquil trailed behind.

"I have news. Who all is here?"

"Everyone," Rosemary walked over and grabbed Cami's left hand, flipping it over. She gave Cami a disdainful glance. "I thought you said you had news." She shifted her gaze to Vince. "You had her alone in another city overnight and didn't get anywhere after your talk earlier this week?"

Vince merely grinned, making Cami nervous. Because he was listening in, she didn't have the guts to give the response she wanted to—that she was far too smart to become engaged to someone she'd only known for a couple months, no matter how she might feel about him—so she settled on rolling her eyes. "Get a grip." She looked at Jonquil. "You have a big mouth, you know that?"

"I'm biding my time," Vince said. "She's not ready yet."

"Hello? News, remember?" Cami said as she set down her packages. She shot a look at Rosemary. "After that crack, you don't deserve to see the new T-strap pumps I bought, or these gorgeous boots."

"Boots? You can't say something like that and not share." Rosemary crossed her arms over her chest.

Cami glanced at Vince. "It's a girl thing."

He shook his head as if still clueless about the fetish.

Lana came to the top of the stairs and headed their way. "Did I hear the words new boots? And what news? Go sit down."

Cami found the rest of her sisters, along with Blake and Joel, sitting in the great room. So it really was nearly everyone.

"Is this a business meeting I shouldn't attend?" Vince asked.

"Join us," Blake said. "I'd rather have you in on the conversation this time."

Vince grinned and grabbed the loveseat, pulling Cami down beside him. She squealed slightly, but settled in. "I appreciate that," he said to Blake.

When everyone was finally seated, Cami started. "So the party last night, while mostly boring and obnoxious, did yield some good results, I think. I spoke with the prince's cousin and he said he would pass along the good word."

"We already received confirmation that the prince's representative is going to be here for the gala," Lana confirmed. "It came a few hours ago."

"Beautiful!" Cami was glad to have good results from the hellish night of socializing.

"I understand you had words with Trent last night," Lana said.

Huh? How did she know? "Yeah. He was being petty, but I think I came out ahead, so we're good."

"You told him you were proud of your sisters and backed us all the way," Jonquil said. "I didn't know you felt that way." Her voice was soft, filled with pleased surprise.

"You heard that?" A few months ago Cami would have sworn this place was like the bottom of a hole, and yet gossip still managed to travel fast.

"There was an interesting article in the news today recapping the conversation you had with Trent, speculating about your former relationship with him," Blake said.

"You didn't send me a link?" Cami asked, feeling a little let down that everyone basically knew everything she had to say and also worried about what was in the article.

"I wanted to talk to you first. I'll send it over tonight."

"Anything else?" Delphi asked. "Because I need to go next while we're all sitting here."

"Yeah, I guess that's it." Cami tried to ignore her feelings of disappointment.

Delphi met her eye. "We wanted you to know most of us have invited our parents to the opening party. I know you're still struggling with what Dad did, and we don't blame you, but we thought we ought to give you time to adjust to the idea of them being here." She added Lana in her gaze.

As Cami looked around at the others, she could see they were all a bit anxious about her response. "I guess this is a night for non-revelatory revelations." She let her mouth quirk. "I already knew."

"Me too," Lana added. "Cami told me a while ago."

"I've studied the guest list several times, checking to see who was coming. I know I've been pretty standoffish, but I'll be happy to welcome them here and treat them with the respect they deserve as your parents." It was hard to hold back the unhappiness she felt as she spoke, but Cami took a moment to look around the circle, catching everyone's gaze. "You should all be proud of what you've accomplished, and what you're making of this hotel. Your parents should share in it, so I'm glad they're coming."

It cost Cami to say the words, and she knew it would take her a while to completely push her bitterness to the background, but she was glad their parents would be able to come. For herself, she felt a strange mixture of relief and regret that her mother was dead and couldn't be there. It would have been great to have her present, to feel the pride her mother always took in her daughters' accomplishments. On the other hand, there would have been pain too, as her mother saw the other women and knew the other four sisters existed because her husband had cheated.

Which still begged the question of whether her mother knew about the other sisters, or about her husband's many affairs.

"Well, that simplifies things," Delphi said.

"Anything else?"

When no one else spoke up, Vince broke the silence. "Great. I better get home, then." He stood, pulling Cami to her feet. "Walk me to the door?"

"She gets all the lip locks," Rosemary complained as they walked away. "It's so not fair."

"Don't take too long," Lana called out. "I want to see those pumps."

Cami laughed, feeling for the first time in months like she really belonged.

CHAPTER 33

A headache pounded behind Cami's left eye as she looked at her overflowing inbox. She hadn't checked her email in almost twenty-four hours, but hadn't expected such an influx. She scanned the messages for anything pressing and her eyes caught one from Liesel Gentry from the transplant database.

Her stomach cramped up when she saw the subject: "Good news!"

She could only imagine it referred to them finding a match for Robert Grady. Yeah, that was good news, but Cami wasn't in a place emotionally to feel good about anything that would make Matilda Grady happy. She pinched the bridge of her nose and closed her eyes for a long moment, trying to center herself. After a moment, she lifted her gaze back to the monitor and clicked the email.

Camellia, great news, I know you were anxious to hear about Robert Grady's results, and we're in luck! We've found a match in Albuquerque. They had enough tests done previously that we can fast-track the transplant. I'm contacting you because you offered to help with travel expenses for the transplant, something I know the Gradys need with the other bills piling up. If you're still able to help us out

224

with this, please let me know and we can discuss the financial aspects of the situation.

Cami felt her throat clog with hot tears as she thought about her commitment to assist with fundraising or even paying for some of the expenses herself. She had been more than happy to make the offer at the time, but her feelings were completely different now. How was she supposed to help the Gradys after everything that had happened?

Blake walked into Cami's office while she stared at a small print of Vincent van Gogh's Starry Night that hung near the door. Cami focused on Blake and tried to put her mind back into work mode.

"Hey," he said, taking the chair across from her. "These pages came to my fax." He handed some papers to her. "And . . ." His brow furrowed. "You're really pale. Are you feeling all right?"

Cami cupped the back of her neck with her hand and looked at him. She didn't really want to talk about it, but he was there and had a look of understanding and compassion. "It's about Robert Grady."

He sat forward, anxious. "What about him? You haven't heard from Matilda, have you?"

"No. I . . ." She let out a breath. "Several weeks ago I managed to track down a new transplant database that holds lists of people who are willing to do organ donations. I got a form for Robert to have his records sent there. Today I opened an email from the director saying they found a match."

His brows pulled together and he frowned. "Why did they contact you? I mean, it was nice and all, but with HIPAA regulations and everything, isn't that odd?"

Cami pursed her lips. "It would be, but when I contacted them, I said that I would help with transportation costs for the donor and arrange lodgings while they were in the area. So Liesel contacted me, but now I'm not feeling nearly so generous."

"That's understandable. Matilda's betrayal is hard on all of you girls—especially you if you were helping her out like that." Blake sat back in the chair and gave her a steady look. "Okay, I don't want to get your back up, but I'm going to play devil's advocate for a moment. Do you think Robert knew about his wife's spying?"

She allowed herself a moment to consider, but based on how Mrs. Grady had talked when she was arrested, she didn't think so. "No."

"Did you think he needed your help before?"

"Yes, but—"

"Do you think he deserves the transplant less than before?"

Cami's jaw tightened as the emotions roiled inside her. It took her several seconds to answer. "No."

"So are you going to punish him because his wife was so desperate to dig their way out of debt that she betrayed you?"

"I thought you were just playing devil's advocate. This sounds like more." She shot him a hard look, but felt tears rising in her eyes.

His gaze held hers for a long moment. "You have every reason to be upset with Matilda, to be angry and feel betrayed. But I want you to think about why you helped out in the first place and decide if you still believe you were right."

There was a long moment of silence as Cami struggled with his question. "I know in my head what happened shouldn't affect things for Robert. Feeling that way is another matter."

"We could always find someone else to head up fundraising efforts, but try to let your head do some of the talking," he suggested. "It's really easy to listen to hurt feelings and not consider all of the details." A sad, faraway look came into his eye and his mouth turned down in frustration.

Cami couldn't help but comment on his reaction, which obviously had nothing to do with their current discussion. "Are you talking about what happened between you and Lana?"

His brows lifted. "What did she tell you about us?"

"Nothing. But I see the way you two bump off of each other. I know you used to be friends, at least, and now she's royally pissed about something."

His lips twitched, as though he were trying to smile, but failed. Sadness filled his eyes. "I can't talk about it if she doesn't want to tell you, but you're on the right track." He turned the picture of Cami and Lana that sat on the edge of her desk and stared at it.

"You love her." Cami was surprised, then wondered why she hadn't seen it from the beginning. She'd wondered if they'd had a relationship, but she hadn't thought it ever got this far.

His gaze flashed to hers. "Yeah, I do."

She desperately wanted to ask if Lana loved him and what had happened, but he'd already said he wouldn't discuss it, so she didn't push—him. Lana was another issue. "Well, whatever happened, I hope you can work things out with her."

"I will. Eventually." But his expression wasn't nearly as certain as his words.

Now that Vince knew what he was competing with to keep Cami in Juniper Ridge, he found it nearly impossible to get time alone with her. They had already begun training new employees, and she worked fourteen-, sometimes sixteen-hour days putting the finishing touches on the hotel, and tracking all of the contractors as they installed equipment and making sure it worked. Then there were the linens to unpack, wash and spread on the beds, the alarm clocks to test, add batteries to and set, and the thousands of inventory items that had to be catalogued and organized.

It made his head spin.

The first five days after their return from Chicago, all Vince managed was to reach her for a couple of quick phone calls, and once he caught her on the grounds while he prepped the yard and she ran between her car and the hotel. He stopped her for a kiss and heard her brief apologies for all but ignoring him. He knew this was temporary and wasn't mad at her for being so busy, but he missed her.

It was late August, and while things were slowing down at the nursery, they were still in the swing of peak season for the landscaping end of things. After taking two days off to run to Chicago with Cami, Vince had to put in plenty of long days to catch up on his own work.

Still, he searched for an elusive hour alone with her.

A week after returning from Chicago, he finished putting his equipment away as the sun dropped out of sight. It would be dark before he caught up with Cami at the hotel, but it was past time she took a breather.

After several queries, he found her making beds on the

228

fourth floor. She looked exhausted in her figure-hugging jeans and a company-logoed, white polo shirt. Cami and Lana worked on opposite sides of the bed, tucking and smoothing as they went, chatting about some snag Lana had dealt with earlier.

"Well, well. You've gone from the board room to becoming maids?" he teased as he appreciated the way Cami's jeans hugged her rear end when she bent over.

Lana flashed a grin at him. "We've both made our share of hotel beds. We started out in housekeeping when we were only fourteen."

He felt his brows lift. "You two are always a bundle of surprises, but you certainly look like you know what you're doing."

Cami plumped a pillow and snugged it at the top of the bed. "If practice makes perfect, half my staff is going to be very good at all kinds of jobs around this place. We've been cross-training everyone, but decided to take on a couple of rooms to refresh our skills." She pushed the auburn curls back from her face as she turned to him.

He crossed the room in two steps and pulled her into his arms. "You're ready to drop. When was the last time you ate?"

When she had to stop and think about it, he knew it had been too long.

"I had lunch." She checked her watch and groaned. "Eight hours ago. No wonder I'm ready to collapse."

"You too?" he asked Lana over Cami's shoulder.

She shook her head. "We all stopped to eat a couple of hours back, but Cami was in the middle of a conference call. I didn't realize she didn't break for dinner after she finished."

Vince rubbed his thumb over Cami's cheek, noticing the

dark circles under her eyes. The worry lines by her mouth were more pronounced too. He was dying to cover her mouth with his. "Unless you object, I'm stealing her, feeding her and putting her to bed early." He said this to Lana, but didn't take his eyes off Cami's face.

"Since she stayed until nearly eleven last night and was back at it by six this morning, I think that's a great idea," Lana answered.

"Oh, but I have so many things to do still," Cami objected.

Vince quieted her with his mouth. When he had her full attention, he pulled back. "I think you just got an order from your boss."

"It wasn't an order," Cami said.

"Oh, yes it was." Lana adjusted the ponytail of red hair at her nape. "In fact, I'm going to insist everyone go home shortly. We're all worn out."

"But there are still stacks of supplies in my office area, and inventory to do—"

Cami kept speaking as Vince scooped her into his arms and headed for the elevator. He called over his shoulder to Lana. "I'll have her back here around seven." Eleven hours wasn't nearly long enough, but he'd take what he could get.

"Sounds fine. See you later."

Cami continued to object, weakly, until the elevator doors shut behind them and he kissed her again. "You ought to let me down. Otherwise people will think I'm sick," she muttered against his mouth.

"Who cares what they think?"

"Mmm. I have to work with them, Vince."

Regretfully, he let her slide down until her feet touched the floor. "If you say so." He lifted his head when the elevator doors opened and he released her before they stepped into the foyer.

Twenty minutes later they were at his house, a bag of takeout on the counter, and Cami was a puddle of exhaustion on his sofa.

Vince brought in a plate with the chicken sandwich and fries he'd ordered for her and set it on the coffee table.

"I shouldn't eat so much. I'm going to grow into a whale," she protested as she swirled fries in ketchup.

"If you spent all day running from one end of the hotel to the next, I don't think gaining weight is going to be a problem. Eat before you fall asleep where you sit."

She shifted her feet to the floor so he could sit beside her and they talked about the day while they polished off the food.

Having her in his home gave the place an air of comfort. Cami drove away the loneliness and just seeing her shoes kicked off by the front door made it feel more lived in, more real. Vince thought of the ring he had tucked away in a drawer upstairs and considered bringing it down to her, but she was too tired to think right now. While that could work to his advantage, he didn't want to ask her to marry him while she was like this. It wasn't fair. And he wasn't sure yet that she'd say yes.

When Cami had eaten most of the food on her plate and her eyes drooped, Vince cleared everything away and took her hand, leading her upstairs. There wouldn't be time or energy for anything but sleeping tonight, but holding her in his arms would be good enough.

231

CHAPTER 34

"You're awfully well rested, considering you spent the night at Vince's," Rosemary observed when Cami walked into the boardroom for the usual eight o'clock meeting.

"Poor guy. I think I was snoring before my head hit the pillow. The last thing I remember was eating dinner and him leading me up the stairs." Cami felt her face warm, though she managed to control her expression.

"I could have sworn he had other plans," Lana teased as Blake sat beside her.

Joel and Sage came in, taking the last chairs between Delphi and Jonquil. The head of engineering crammed in the far corner.

"Sometimes," Blake said, "looks are deceiving."

Lana's face tightened. "And sometimes they aren't."

"O-kay, if we can change the subject back to something relevant." Cami didn't want people discussing her private life at the meeting. She glanced at Rosemary, whose eyes darted to Lana and Blake, then back to Cami, and her brows quirked in question. Cami lifted her shoulders to show her confusion.

Lana started the meeting with the day's company message, before shooting right into what still needed to be accomplished. They would have guests on the premises in three days, after all, and the to-do list barely seemed to have shrunk at all.

Thursday night Lana sent everyone home and locked up the hotel for the last time. Security did one last sweep to make sure the place was empty and left a couple of guys to patrol the halls overnight.

Cami called a gathering at the house, including Blake and all of the other department heads, the main chefs, head of housekeeping and assistant managers of each department along with their significant others, which meant Vince was by her side.

They ate takeout, hashed over plans for the next day, and mingled for over an hour before people started to leave to get a good night's sleep.

When the rest of the department heads left the sisters, Joel, Blake, Harrison, Alex, and Vince at the house, Cami sent Vince to her room to get the package that had arrived from Tiffany's a few days earlier. As he came back down the stairs, she called everyone to order. "I know that at work Lana is the boss, but as I'm now the oldest member of the family—" she pointed at Alex. "You don't count this time, sorry—I decided it was my job to step up, at least tonight." She took the box from Vince and clutched it to her. Her mouth was dry from nerves, and she felt more emotional than she cared to admit.

"It's been a rough summer and we didn't exactly come together under the most ideal circumstances." That brought a round of chuckles. "But I have to let you all know how proud I am of you." She paused as her voice broke. "How proud Dad would have been of all of us. It's going to take a while for us to adjust, to figure out how we all work together, but I feel like we're already starting to mesh, despite the inevitable rough spots along the way."

Jonquil flashed one of her infectious smiles. "And if we don't mesh, Rosemary will step in and straighten us out."

"You got that right," Rosemary put in.

Cami felt the knot in her stomach start to loosen. "Anyway, during my trip to Chicago a couple of weeks ago, I realized despite all of his many, many mistakes, Dad had the right idea putting us together. And I think we make a pretty awesome team. The media has been trying to tear us apart, destroy the family name, but it's not about them, it's about us, and what we can accomplish when we stick together." She saw tears in Lana's eyes.

"Hear, hear!" This came from Blake.

Vince snaked an arm around Cami's waist and gave her a squeeze of support.

"So, I wanted to commemorate what we've accomplished here and send a message of unity to anyone who sees us. We're sisters. We stick together, and no one is going to count us out." She fumbled with the jewelry boxes, setting them onto the counter as she spoke. "I discussed options with the jeweler for a while before we came up with the right thing. I got one for each of us. Don't open them until everyone has one."

Cami's hands shook as she passed the boxes around to her sisters, then returned to her spot beside Vince and picked up her own. "I decided a lapel pin was the most sensible option, considering our various uniforms. Open them."

There were gasps as the women checked out the gold stylized letter D from the DiCarlo Hotels logo, but on the D the jewelers had inscribed leaves and flowers with the sister's birth stone inserted in the upper corner of the letter. "It was a delicate balance, trying to find something feminine enough for Sage without being too girly for Rosemary."

Lana fingered hers. "Wow, you worked with Xavier to design this, didn't you?"

"You know your jewelers," Cami said, chuckling.

"He's the best there is."

"It's like a little bouquet, but it looks almost like etchings, a nice touch," Jonquil said, then listed each plant as her finger slid along the letters' curve.

There was more banter as everyone tried on the pins and talked about getting together for a group picture on the grounds as soon as Jeremy arrived to start snapping photos.

"I think that's our cue to leave you ladies," Alex said, grabbing his briefcase. "But first, I have something else for you." He pulled out a stack of long business envelopes and tapped them in his hand, studying each of their faces. "I know George would be proud of all of you tonight regardless of how tomorrow goes. You've all come through." He passed them around before he, Joel, Blake and Harrison left.

Cami felt many different emotions zooming through her as she held the envelope, unsure whether she wanted to read it. Vince put an arm around her shoulders. "Walk me to my car?"

"Yeah." She snuggled closer as they exited the house and crossed the yard to where he'd parked his Mustang.

"I think the pins were a hit," he said, nuzzling her temple and pressing a kiss beside her ear.

"It seems that way. I know we've got a long way to go before we become the team Dad wanted—if we ever do. And who knows where we'll all be in a little over a year. What's the chance people like us will hang around here once the will has been satisfied?" She hadn't thought much about leaving since she and Vince had started to grow close. But she'd never really considered staying in Colorado. It wasn't home to her; it was snowy for most of the year, and cold and windy. She supposed compared to Chicago, those weren't big considerations. But it was...not Chicago. Not the place where she had grown up and worked most of her adult life. It wasn't where she planned to be.

And now she had to question what she wanted and where she would end up, because Chicago held much less attraction for her than Juniper Ridge did. Or maybe it was just the man who had his arm around her shoulders. He was always there for her, her support, a listening ear, the one she could lean on when things were rough, and he never asked for more than she could give. When she compared him to Trent—to anyone she had dated before—they just couldn't compare.

Vince pulled her close and pressed a kiss to her mouth so slow and drugging, she stopped thinking altogether.

When he released her, Cami looked up into his eyes and knew this was love. The strong kind that lasted decades. She kissed him once more, wanting to show him what he meant to her, even if the realization had made her too breathless to speak.

Vince tipped his forehead against hers. "I'd be willing to bet a few of the sisters will fall in love with the area before their time is up here."

Cami didn't get a chance to tell him she thought he was right before he kissed her again.

CHAPTER 35

When Cami came back inside, Delphi was the only one in sight. She sat at the table, the opened jeweler's box and unopened letter sitting before her. "I don't know how I feel about all of this," Delphi said after glancing in Cami's direction.

"That's okay. I didn't expect you to jump for joy and want to be my best buddy ever. Dad threw us all for a loop."

"What happened?" Delphi turned all the way so she could look Cami in the eye. "When we first got here, I thought you were the least happy about things. You held back more than anyone else. And now suddenly you want us all to be super-close sisters?" There were dark hollows under her eyes. Everyone was worn out from the long weeks of preparation, but there was something more to this than weariness.

Cami slid into a nearby chair and pulled her letter out of her back pocket, fingering it. "I don't expect an overnight transformation. I don't think Dad's vision of all of us being close and supporting each other for the rest of our lives is possible—not the way he wanted it."

Delphi nudged the Tiffany's box. "Then what's with the matching pins?"

"Two parts. First, I decided to let go of whatever anger I felt for you guys just for existing. I'm still mad at Dad. But, it's not your fault, and I'm not going to hold it against you anymore."

After a long stare, Delphi nodded. "I'd appreciate that. It hasn't been all hugs and puppies for us, either, you know."

"And second," Cami drew in a breath. "I believe in us. I want to send a message of solidarity; we're strong, and we're going to make this happen. As long as we work as a team, no one is going to stop us."

Delphi looked back at the letter on the table and took another sip of her drink. "What do you think this round of letters says? I'm not sure if I dare open it."

Cami felt the smooth heavy-bond paper as she ran her fingers over it. "I know. I can't help but wonder if he thought these letters were supposed to make us all feel better about his decisions. And since part of me doesn't *want* to forgive him, I'm torn over whether or not I should read it."

Delphi finished off her glass in one gulp, then stood from the bar. "No one said we have to read them tonight." She slid the letter and pin from the counter. "We have a long few days ahead of us. Better get some rest."

"Yeah. Good night." Before heading up the stairs to her room, Cami watched Delphi walk away. Cami shut the door behind her and dropped her letter and pin on the dresser before beginning her bedtime routine.

When she lay in bed, she picked up the letter again and stared at it in the lamplight. On one hand, she wanted to know what her father had to say. She missed having him there to turn to, and tomorrow was a huge day for them all. On the other side of the spectrum was the worry that whatever he said may not satisfy her.

Cami,

If you're reading this, you took the job at the hotel, and you're opening it tomorrow. I'm sure the past couple of months have been full of pitfalls and struggles. Opening a hotel is a big job, but one I found immensely rewarding. The only thing I regretted about the fifteen I opened in my career was that it took me away from my girls so often.

I know it's too much to hope that you and your sisters have become automatic friends, but I hope the past few months have put things into motion for you all to create close friendships before the year is out. Cami, you're a leader—the one I see coming out as the head of the family, even though Lana will be the boss at the hotel, and Rosemary has a personality strong enough to turn any parent's hair gray. Leadership is a funny thing, isn't it? The harder you push people to follow, the more they go their own way, but the more acceptance and friendship you offer, the more they fall in line.

The next year is bound to be a difficult one, but you have the ability to lead softly, to pull people to you, which will come in handy both at work and at home.

But don't forget that there's so much more to life than work. You tend to forget that a social life—one including people you enjoy being around, not the staid relationships that make up the upper crust—is important. Get out, meet people, make true connections. And know whatever happens, I love all my girls more than life, and I want you to be happy. Focus on that, and the rest will work out for itself.

All my love,
Dad

Cami bit her lip as she wiped away tears. She missed having him there to share jokes and dreams. Though she hadn't forgiven him yet, she knew she was on her way. Whatever else he might have done, she knew he loved his girls.

That meant something now.

Breakfast the next morning was crazy with everyone rushing to prepare and popping in and out of the kitchen. When Cami came down, ready to go and wondering if her stomach would hold any food, she found Sage sitting at the table, the newspaper open in front of her. "What news from the astrology section today?" she asked as she grabbed a banana from a bunch on the counter.

Sage studied the paper. "Yours promises an encounter with an old flame that will put everything into perspective."

Cami smiled. "Ah, that could be interesting The question is which perspective . . . " She looked up and saw Lana descending the stairs. "What about for her?"

"What astrological sign are you?" Sage asked Lana.

"I don't believe those things," Lana dismissed.

"Just play along," Cami said. "You know the paper promised me love the day we met Vince in the park. It might be entertaining to see what it offers for you."

"Funny." Despite that, Lana called back over her shoulder to Sage, "I'm a Scorpio."

"Ah, that explains so much," Sage said, then stopped with her finger on a paragraph in the paper. "Today is your lucky day, the beginning of something new and special. Allow love a chance and your life will be changed."

"Right. Love is so not happening. I could use a lucky day, though. I think we all could." Lana poured herself a glass of cranberry juice and leaned back against the counter to sip it.

"Who needs luck," Jonquil asked as she joined them in the kitchen. "We've worked our tails off. This is going to go off without a hitch."

"You said it," Rosemary said as she and Delphi came into the room.

"Everyone ready?" Delphi asked as she slung her bag over her shoulder. "We've got some serious butt to kick."

Cami grabbed the paper on her way out the door, scanning it as she got into the car with Lana. When her eyes landed on the horoscope page, though, she was surprised to see that other than the bit about the lucky day, Sage's predictions were different than what the paper said. Weird. When she remembered the time Sage had predicted the Fourth of July would be full of surprises—and not necessarily good ones, Cami paused. She dismissed the thought. No one could know things like that.

The first arrivals weren't expected until at least ten o'clock, but the hotel hummed with activity by eight, excitement and nerves mounting as the employees prepared for opening day.

Nearly all of the sisters lent a hand in the first hours, ensuring everything was in place until Delphi said she couldn't think of another thing that needed to be done. Cami questioned her staff members, making sure they had answers to all of the usual questions and a number of the less common ones. She checked and double-checked all of the details under her control and probably drove everyone near her crazy.

And then guests started to arrive and everything clicked along as Cami oversaw her employees while they began the check-in procedures that were so familiar to her.

It turned out Zelda Gifford was a statuesque blonde—definitely aided by a salon—even taller than her daughter and as slender as a flower stem. Cami thought Delphi was a classy mixture of her mother and father, getting the best of both worlds in many ways.

Zelda checked to make sure her room was hypoallergenic and there would be no fresh flowers in there—she was allergic, after all—and was her appointment at the spa still on? She verified her spot at the gala dinner that night—she had to be sure she was seated close so she could hear the speakers if something went terribly awry with the audio system. Cami was grateful the woman was Delphi's problem and not her own.

Cami's exasperation at the woman's pickiness outshone her twisted emotions as she spoke with Zelda. "I hope you have a nice weekend. Delphi has been working very hard to get everything ready. You must be so proud of her."

"Well, yes, of course," Zelda said in a tone that indicated she didn't see why she should be. "Delphi always did have her own way of doing things. Her father always encouraged her to do whatever she wanted." This last held more than a little distaste.

"He was always good about supporting our interests," Cami agreed, forcing her smile to stay in place as her dislike for the woman grew. "If you need some help with your bags, Jeffery's free to assist you."

"Oh, yes, thank you. I do need a nap before my massage." She waggled her fingers at Jeffery. "Come along, then."

Cami prayed the other sisters had gotten much luckier in the mom department, then she wondered what her father had ever seen in Zelda—surely he'd gone for more than just a pretty face, hadn't he?

Sage's mother—"Just call me Darla, honey"—may have

been eccentric, but fortunately, she was completely sweet. Jonquil's mother was a tiny brunette with flashing blue eyes like her daughter's and despite George's having taken good care of her financially, she took in the hotel with avid curiosity, saying she'd never stayed anywhere so fancy. Cami liked her immensely.

Rosemary's mother didn't come at all, which brought up all kinds of questions Cami didn't have time to ask.

Things were going along smoothly and Cami was starting to think the whole event would go off without a hitch when Trent and Trina arrived. She'd noticed Trina's name on the guest list but hoped the two of them would arrive and check in while she was busy elsewhere. She would have managed to avoid them for a while if Trent hadn't requested to speak with her.

Cami put on her best social face and came out with a smile, nerves filling her stomach. "Trent, Trina, I'm so glad you made it. This is going to be a great weekend!"

"This is lovely. You've done such an amazing job," Trina said, her voice completely sincere. "You must be so pleased."

"Yes, and we're completely booked, which is always nice."

"If we wander around here for a while, I suppose we'll see all of your dad's carbon copies," Trent said, gesturing with his hands.

Cami fought to not grind her teeth. "I'm sure you'll run into one or two of my sisters during the weekend, but I wouldn't say we look much alike. It makes for a diverse and interesting group with lots to offer." She wished she dared shut him down for his bad behavior, and noticed the way Trina's brows furrowed in unhappiness at his comments. Cami imagined how Rosemary would have responded. She would have to be content with that image, however false because responding that way would be a mistake.

"I'm sure Cami has a lot to do today," Trina said, giving Trent's arm a tug. "We'll get a chance to talk to you later."

Cami was happy to see them walk away.

CHAPTER 36

Cami brought her formal dress for the gala with her to work that morning, so after a quick double-check of her department that afternoon, she took her dress upstairs to Lana's office to change and fix her makeup in the executive restroom.

"Has Joel had any more luck tracking the payments into Mrs. Grady's account?" she asked Lana as she touched up her mascara.

"No, he said the payments were made in cash. He has extra guys working tonight to make sure everything goes off without a hitch. I doubt anything's going to happen, but with our luck lately, you never know."

"No kidding." Cami eyed her sister in the mirror. "How are you holding up?"

"Fine. Shouldn't I be? Everything's going like clockwork." She didn't meet Cami's gaze.

"I wonder if Rosemary and Delphi would say it's going like clockwork. They're the ones in the thick of the last-minute preparations for tonight."

"Better them than me, for sure."

Cami pulled out her favorite lipstick and faced the mirror. "So tell me what happened between you and Blake."

Lana froze as she touched up her mascara. It only lasted a second, but when she started moving and responded, her voice was a little strained. "What do you mean?"

"I mean something's up between you. It's obvious. You act like you used to be a couple, but you're trying to pretend you barely know each other."

"I don't know what you're talking about. We're only colleagues."

Cami considered telling Lana that Blake admitted to loving her, but decided to keep that to herself. If it was told in confidence, she'd respect that. For now, anyway. "You have history of a romantic nature, don't you?" She pressed her lips together and checked to make sure her lipstick was straight.

Lana stared at the counter as she put all of her cosmetics back into a bag. "I don't want to talk about Blake and me. It's over and done with. Maybe we can talk about it another day."

Though Cami figured Lana was hoping to make 'another day' into never, she took the hint for now. The next few hours would be filled with enough stress without forcing Lana to hash out her relationship history.

Blake and Vince waited in the main office when the women emerged. Cami had to bite her lip in appreciation when she saw them—both looked completely fabulous, though of course, she only flashed her gaze over Blake before zeroing in on Vince. "You both look great."

"Not half as great as you two." Vince handed her a bouquet of calla lilies.

"Thanks, they're perfect." Cami gave him a kiss hello.

"I was considering a corsage, but Jonquil said no. Was she right?" Vince slid an arm around her waist and led her toward the stairwell.

"Never doubt Jonquil when it comes to flowers." She rubbed the silky petals against her cheek and inhaled the weak floral scent.

After depositing the bouquet in her office, the four of them continued into the ballroom for the gala. Cami noticed the way Lana kept her hands to herself, but allowed Blake to guide her with a hand at her back.

Though Cami was busy talking to people and handling details Delphi threw her way, Vince stayed with her, apparently content to just be by her side. The same easy confidence he'd exhibited other times they had attended parties shone through as the evening progressed.

The dinner and ribbon cutting went well and the dancing had just begun when Vince pulled Cami into his arms and maneuvered her onto the floor. "How are you doing?" he asked, his voice low in her ear.

"Great." She'd spoken to dozens of people, smiled like it was pasted on, and wanted nothing more than to go for a quiet walk in the cool evening air where she and Vince could be alone for a while. She wondered if they could slip out for a while. Her phone started to vibrate and she pulled it out to find the number from the front desk. "Sorry. Just a minute."

"This is Cami," she said.

"Hi, this is Kristi. I have a problem with one of the check-ins and neither of us can figure it out. I'm really sorry. I know you're busy."

Though she wanted to sigh, Cami just smiled in resignation. "Sure, I'll be right there." She ended the call and turned to Vince in apology. "I just have a little check-in problem. It should only take a few minutes. I'm sorry."

He lifted his hand and brushed his thumb along her jaw.

"No problem. How about if I get us some food? You probably haven't eaten in hours."

Her stomach *was* feeling pretty empty and despite the fact that she was in a major social engagement—which usually zapped her appetite—she thought she could eat something. "That sounds great."

Getting back through the crowd quickly was a test in social grace, but in only a couple of minutes Cami made it out of the ballroom and headed to the foyer. The sound of the band fell behind her and she appreciated the cooler air now she was away from all the people. Her heels clicked on the marble floor tiles and she smiled as though she hadn't a care in the world, though her feet were already throbbing. A glance at the shoes she'd bought while she and Vince had been in Chicago reminded her that the pain was well worth it. They looked fabulous!

"Hi," she greeted the older couple when she reached the registration desk. "I'm Cami DiCarlo. Let's see if we can figure out what's going on here." She came around the counter and let Kristi fill her in on the problem.

After a few minutes she corrected the issue and sent the guests on their way, then ran through the problem with both of the service experts so they would know how to fix it next time. She was nearly finished when she glanced up and saw Trent going up the staircase to the second floor.

She finished reviewing procedures with the girls, but kept sneaking peeks at the staircase. There wasn't anything up there except convention space and the executive offices. Trent would probably follow the winding hall and end up at the other staircase.

Vince walked over to her, a plate of food in his hand, and smiling. "I wondered if you were about done here."

"All finished." She said goodnight to the girls and took Vince's elbow. "Can we take a quick detour on our way back to the ballroom?"

"Sure." He lifted a stuffed mushroom cap to her mouth and fed it to her.

The flavors burst on her tongue and she sighed with appreciation. "Wow. Remind me to tell Rosemary how amazing she is."

"There's more where that came from." His voice was barely more than a low rumble, but it made her shiver. Or maybe that was due to the light brush of his hand along her spine through the thin fabric of her dress.

"I can't wait to try them all."

His gaze practically sizzled in the air as he looked at her. "If there are extras, we might have to take some back to my place to celebrate privately."

"I think I could get behind that." She was grateful for his steadying presence as they ascended the stairs.

He turned her around and backed her against the wall once they were out of sight of guests. She melted into him. "I've never been so glad to get away from a crowd before." She lifted her mouth to his and savored the kiss for a long moment.

"Mmmm. I should have brought you up here a while ago. Maybe we could duck into your office for a few minutes." His mouth glided along her jaw to her ear. "I've wanted to get you alone since I saw you in this dress."

"Now's not the time." She shivered as his breath fluttered against her neck and his lips teased the sensitive skin beneath her earlobe. "I have people downstairs I'm supposed to mingle with."

"Duty never ends."

"Isn't that the truth?" Her eyes flashed over the glass doors into the executive offices and she thought she saw movement. She stopped and stared as a shadow crossed in front of the door to Lana's office. "What's going on?"

"What?" Vince asked, glancing behind him.

"Hold on." Cami moved to the glass doors that led into the offices and pushed one open. It wasn't locked as she thought they had left it earlier.

"It's probably just Lana, come back to pick up something," Vince said, but he kept his voice pitched low.

"Yeah." Still, Cami wasn't sure she believed it.

Vince slid the plate of hors d'oeuvres onto the office manager's desk, and led the way to Lana's door. He twisted the handle and opened it quickly.

Trent stood on the other side, riffling through some papers. He glanced up in surprise at the sound of the door opening.

"What are you doing here?" Cami asked.

CHAPTER 37

Trent's eyes grew wide and his mouth dropped open for just a second before he covered it with a smooth smile. "Hey, Lana asked me to drop some papers up here." He circled back around the desk. "You have a really nice hotel, did I mention that earlier? You must be so pleased with how everything is going tonight."

"Yes, it's been great." Cami crossed her arms over her chest and stared him down. "What are you really doing up here? The room was locked."

A flicker of anger erupted on Trent's face, yet it vanished almost as quickly as it had appeared. A congenial smile flashed onto his face and he moved toward them. "How about if we head back down to the party?"

Vince grabbed Trent by the arm as he tried to waltz by. "Not so fast. The lady asked you a question and you need to answer it."

"Hey, get your hands off, lawn boy. I'm not doing anything wrong." Trent tried to pull his arm out of Vince's grip, but ended up with it twisted high behind his back.

"Then how did you get in here?" Cami pulled her cell phone out of her pocket and speed dialed Joel.

"The door was open."

"I checked that lock myself. I know it was locked." She looked at him, disgusted. "You're a terrible liar, Trent. I have no idea how I never saw it before."

His blue eyes flashed at her. "You saw what you wanted to see."

"Hey, Joel," Cami said when he picked up. "We have an intruder in Lana's office. Could you come up here?" He stated he would and they hung up.

"Who did you call?" Trent asked.

"Our head of security. He has a knack for getting to the bottom of things." Cami leaned back against the desk and looked at Trent, whose face was turning red from anger. "Tell me, Trent, what else have you been up to lately?"

His eyes darkened and his jaw hardened. "I don't know what you're talking about."

"Really?" Vince twisted Trent's arm more, causing him to suck in a pained breath.

"I think you know what I'm talking about," Cami said. "The news reports, the pictures and rumors. I know you've heard of them."

"Of course. Everyone's heard about them. That doesn't mean I had anything to do with it." Trent winced as Vince gave his arm another yank. "Stop that. I'm not doing anything wrong here."

Cami called Lana and asked her to come up to the office. She would need to take a look through her papers and make sure nothing was missing. When she finished, she looked at Trent again. "How about if you come clean now and save us all a lot of hassle?"

"Right. Because you're one of the mighty DiCarlos, so I should just kowtow and do whatever you want. Follow your rules, accept your decisions. Your father did everything he could to ruin me. It's only by luck that I still have a business."

"He's hardly to blame if he chose to go with a different company. He had to make the right decisions for the hotel chain—regardless of personal relationships." Of course, he'd never liked Trent, and actively tried to convince her to break up. No use mentioning it, though.

He snorted. "Right, what's best for the company, which is why he put his six daughters all to work here—it had nothing to do with personal relationships."

She decided to ignore that as he was both right that the decision had been a personal one, and wrong that it had been a bad move for the business.

The hall door opened and Joel entered the front office with another security guard. Lana and Blake entered in their wake and Alex wasn't far behind.

The second security guard took Trent into the next room while Joel did a sweep for bugs—finding several that hadn't been there last he'd checked. Since the day he'd found the bugs and cameras at their home, Joel had been doing a sweep of each of the sisters' office areas every couple of days, but until now they had been clean. "Looks like we found our problem," he said as he finished Lana's office. "I'll have to do a full sweep of everyone's areas again tonight, just to be sure he didn't manage to sneak in any others. Also, I'll get Mrs. Grady to meet us at the police department for a lineup, see if she recognizes him."

Cami felt faintly ill at the thought that Trent might have been behind everything. She knew he'd been unhappy about their breakup, but she had no idea he could hate like that.

"I know everyone's upset," Alex said after Joel left the office, "but we do still have a party going on downstairs, and an awful lot of the key people are up here instead of there. We really ought to head back down, put on our social smiles, and get through the evening."

He was right, though it didn't make Cami any more excited about returning to the crowd and pretending everything was great. She was glad for Vince's arm around her shoulder as he led her toward the hallway. "Okay, let's get back to it."

"Don't look so excited," Lana teased, following on their heels. "Someone might get the idea that you aren't an avid social climber."

"And that would be a terrible shame." A thought popped into her head and she turned to Lana. "Trina. She's got to be wondering what's happened to Trent by now."

Lana cursed, then let out a huff of irritation. "Right. So who gets that pleasure?"

"I'll take care of it," Alex volunteered, though a glance in his direction showed grim lines bracketed his mouth.

Relief filled Cami as she allowed Vince to lead her back down the staircase. She had barely eaten anything before the confrontation, but though her stomach was still empty, she didn't think she could eat anything more.

CHAPTER 38

Monday night Cami was curled up in an overstuffed chair in the living room, watching Rosemary and Jonquil debate professional basketball teams. Rosemary argued that the Chicago Bulls were hands down the best while Jonquil thought the Seventy-Sixers would beat their socks off this season. Cami didn't really understand the draw of watching people run up and down a court for three hours, but watching her sisters argue was plenty entertaining.

The doorbell rang and Jonquil jumped up to answer it. At the door she turned to face them, "Cami, you have a vis—" her words cut off as an arm came around her neck and a glint of silver lifted to her temple.

Cami felt her throat close off as she recognized the gun only an instant before seeing Trent was the one holding it. Jonquil's blue eyes widened with terror as she looked at all of them. "What's going on?" she asked, her voice high and squeaky.

"Shut up." Trent's arm tightened around her neck, making her bow to the side. "Camellia knows exactly what this is about. Don't you, sweetheart?"

Rosemary and Delphi stood to face him. Cami rose to her feet and glanced to the kitchen where Sage had been only a moment later. She was huddled behind the kitchen island, tears streaming down her frightened face and texting with shaky fingers. Lana was in her room; with any luck, she'd stay there. "Hey, it's going to be okay," Cami said to Jonquil, though her voice quavered, belying the way her heart raced and her hands sweated. "Trent, I heard they released you this morning. You don't want to hurt her. Let her go."

"You really think I'd give up the advantage when I finally have everyone's attention?" He chuckled, but didn't look amused. "Do you know how hard I've worked to get it?"

"What do you want, Trent?" Cami used his name deliberately, hoping it would make him feel in control and calm him.

"A little respect would have been nice. You know, this is all yours and your dad's fault. It didn't have to be this way." His eyes darted, taking in the room around him, but not really settling on anyone.

"Then you can let the others go and just deal with me." The thought of being alone with him while he carried a gun was almost more than she could handle, but Cami couldn't let one of the others get hurt. She was the real target here. "You can tell me exactly where I went wrong and how to fix it."

"What do you think I am, an idiot?" He tightened his arm more around Jonquil's neck, causing her to gasp slightly as her head was yanked back. "Besides, I've decided you're all going to pay—you're all his daughters, sharing in the spoils gained at my expense."

"What are you talking about?" Rosemary asked.

He lifted his thumb and cocked the revolver as he glared at her.

Cami took the second of distraction to dart a glance at

the balcony. She'd seen Lana's auburn curls flash into her periphery, then disappear. Cami really hoped Lana was calling the police. And Joel. His special training had to be an asset right now and the police station was miles away. They just needed to hold Trent off until help could arrive. Was it possible? Would any of them come out of this alive? "Don't do this, Trent. They're not responsible for anything."

"They exist." He shrugged as if that were reason enough. "I should take you all out of the picture, make a clean slate. I should have done that in the first place, just set a bomb to go off while you all slept. The world would be better off without the DiCarlo blood trying to manage and control the world. Your father ruined my life, you know. If he hadn't interfered, I'd be riding high and happy, even if we hadn't gotten married."

Cami must have looked as surprised as she felt because his chuckle held twisted joy. "You didn't actually think I was in love with you, did you? I was trying to get an in with your father so he'd take my contracts, then when he didn't, I figured marrying you so I had access to your fortune would be good enough." His eyes narrowed again. "I don't know what he told you to keep you away from me."

"Nothing." Cami folded her arms across her chest. "I knew he didn't care for you much, but he didn't say why you didn't get the contract. He got sick, acting weird; I was busy worrying about him and juggling work. Then I realized you were being a pushy jerk and decided to end things."

"Cami!" Jonquil's voice was panicked and her voice high pitched. "What are you doing?"

But Cami ignored the question and kept her gaze on Trent. "It wasn't until later, when I told my dad you'd proposed, that I'd accepted, but I'd already called it off that

257

he mentioned there were some underhanded dealings going on and to keep my distance. He never elaborated."

"You're lying. I don't believe it."

"He had a few more important things to worry about—like the fact that he was dying. And trying to juggle visits from six daughters without us finding out about his illness or each other." This last she added with a touch of irony in her voice. Funny how hard he worked to keep them apart while he was alive, only to force them all together the moment he died.

Trent moved farther into the room, stationing himself at the bottom of the stairs. "Whether that's true or not, it doesn't change things." He gave Jonquil's slim neck another yank, causing her to gag slightly as tears poured down her cheeks. "When your father pulled his contracts, I lost everything. He spoke to all the wrong people, people I owed money to, people who had the power to fix my problems. I can't get a contract anymore."

He seemed to enjoy elucidating every perceived slight. "At the gala I was just looking for information. I wasn't going to hurt anyone, but you had to stick your nose where it wasn't wanted."

"You didn't belong in the executive offices. And you've done plenty of sticking your nose where it doesn't belong, lately," Cami pointed out.

"Trina won't have anything to do with me now." Trent's words came out in a growl, his eyes dark and his face harder than Cami had ever seen it before. "She was my ticket out of this mess. That's your fault."

That line of thought was faulty in so many ways, Cami couldn't begin to list them all. She caught movement out the door window and saw Joel peeking in at them, a hand gun in his grip, and a rifle over his shoulder. Then he was gone. It didn't change the fact that Trent had a gun to Jonquil's head, but it did make Cami feel better. They just had to keep his finger from getting twitchy. "I didn't say anything to Trina, but it's not like she wouldn't miss you when you didn't come back. Someone had to tell her what happened to you."

"Who's this Trina chick?" Rosemary asked.

"Shut up. This is between me and Cami," Trent yelled.

"So why won't you let Jonquil go? If it's between us, there's no need to hurt her." Cami took a couple of steps in his direction.

"Stop where you are or I will kill her."

She believed him, but she needed to get just a little closer. "And then your situation will get worse than it is already. Why make it harder for yourself, Trent?"

Lana appeared at the balcony behind him with a softball in her hand. She was amazingly accurate when she threw stuff, but Cami needed to get the gun pointed somewhere else first.

"It's not like I have anything left. You've taken everything from me now. Your whole family is responsible. And you'll all pay. One at a time." A grim smile slid onto his face. "Starting now."

"Everyone get down." Cami lunged for his arm, yanking it away so the shot plowed into the kitchen island. Sage screamed. Lana threw the ball, beaning Trent in the head. Jonquil gave him an elbow in the nose, making blood spurt. Both Joel and Vince pushed through the front and garage entrances, guns out and ready to fire.

"Get down!" Joel yelled. "Drop the weapon!"

Another bullet shot from the revolver and Cami rolled behind the coffee table just before twin blasts filled the air, almost simultaneously.

"Don't you dare move." Joel began swearing heatedly and Cami glanced under the heavy wooden coffee table to see Joel's knee in the middle of Trent's back.

"You shot me." Trent sounded a little dazed.

"No shit, I'm glad you noticed." He paused, turning to Vince. "Get the girls out of here. And call for an ambulance. The creep's going to live, but he'll need his wounds tended."

Cami looked up to see Vince standing over her. She felt wetness on her cheeks, not sure when she started crying.

Vince pulled her up into his arms, wrapping her in a tight, if short embrace. "Hey, baby, are you all right? Are you hurt?"

"I'm fine." Cami felt the loss of his arms as he released her, but pretended not to as she wiped her face. She looked around at all of her sisters, taking stock to see if they were okay.

Sage cried and rocked behind the kitchen island and Cami went over, checking to make sure she was okay.

"Fine. I'm fine. I'm fine." She continued to repeat the words to herself, not responding to Cami's other questions.

Cami looked up to Vince pleadingly, and he took Sage's other elbow so they could get her out of the house.

Joel looked up and saw Sage, his eyes widened and his nostrils flared. "Are you okay?"

Sage's mantra continued.

"She doesn't seem hurt. We'll take care of her," Vince said.

"I'll be out to check when the cops get here."

Vince and Cami pulled Sage toward the door as police officers began pouring into the room. He grabbed Jonquil as they passed, dragging her out as well. Cami glanced back to see a dark red patch on Trent's shoulder, but didn't catch more before Vince led them outside, talking, "Someone is going to come speak to you. They'll probably want to talk to you individually, so don't discuss what happened while you're outside, okay?"

He deposited them both around the corner of the house, out of view of the living room windows and driveway, which was full of police and sheriff's department vehicles. Sirens announced more emergency personnel were on the way. "Stay here and I'll go grab the rest of your sisters." Before he turned away, Vince gave Cami a quick, hard kiss, as if to reassure himself that she was really all right.

A minute later he returned with the rest of the sisters and two officers followed behind them.

"Hi, I'm Deputy Peacock. Did anyone get hurt in there? Any injuries?"

Cami studied her sisters, but though they appeared upset, they all shook their heads. "It looks like we got away with no more than a bruise or two and enough nightmares to hijack our dreams for the next decade." She had her arm around Sage still, who cried into her knees. She looked around and found Jonquil shaking slightly, but she didn't look nearly as upset as Sage—which was confusing, since Jonquil was the one at gunpoint. Her skin, however, looked kind of gray. "Then again, maybe you ought to check her for shock," she gestured to the youngest sister.

Vince pulled Cami close and pressed a kiss to her temple. "Luckily, you're gutsy women and we got here in good time."

It hadn't seemed like good time. It had seemed like forever, but Cami didn't mention it.

The EMTs brought out a blanket, laid Jonquil down and elevated her legs after they took her blood pressure, but after a few minutes she claimed she was feeling better. She refused to go to the hospital, though the rest of them encouraged it.

The officers sat all of them down, separated, with a pen and paper to write their statements in as much detail as they could remember. Sage stopped crying and Joel came out while the rest of them were writing and went to her, kneeling beside her and speaking in low tones. She leaned into him and answered back, her voice soft and shaky, but she seemed to calm faster with him nearby. After a few minutes they each wrote their own version of the events.

CHAPTER 39

"So much for the romantic dinner I had planned," Vince said as he and Cami sat cross-legged on his living room carpet that evening, feasting on fried chicken and potato wedges. Vince had finally gotten a chance to drive her car, taking it out to the police station to meet her, then driving the two of them to the grocery store deli to pick up dinner.

"Did you have a romantic evening planned? You're just full of those, aren't you?" After she'd finished with the police, Cami had taken a long, hot shower and changed into fresh clothes. Though she felt better than before, she was still all knotted up from the day's events. It was just as well Vince changed his mind. Hanging out at his place was exactly her speed right now.

"Well, I had other expectations for Friday night, but then we had a little too much of the wrong kind of excitement. And today—again—things didn't exactly go as I'd hoped." He'd barely let her out of his sight since bursting into her place—he even waited in her room while she showered. "I nearly had a heart attack when Joel snagged me on his way to the car saying Trent was holding Jonquil hostage at gunpoint." He used his knuckle to lift Cami's chin so he could kiss her, then used a napkin to wipe away the chicken grease he'd just smeared on her lips.

Cami had never been so shaken over anything. When she thought of him bursting into the house, his gun raised and ready to protect her, of how easy it would have been for Trent to turn and shoot Vince, it made her chest ache. "No reason tonight can't still be romantic. The dogs are outside; we're in here, eating by candlelight." In his house—which felt more like home with every visit.

"That's true." He changed the subject to something neutral, and the topics wandered while they finished their meal, then topped it off with the Twinkies Cami had grabbed for dessert.

"Don't tell Rosemary I picked out Twinkies. She'd have a fit if she knew I defiled myself with substandard pastries." Cami took a big bite and reveled in the over-processed goodness.

Vince chuckled and dabbed her nose with some of the cream filling from his snack cake. "You got it." He leaned in and kissed the cream away, then moved to her mouth. "You know I'd do anything for you," he whispered against her lips.

"Even come in guns a blazing to save me." She was trying to put it all in perspective.

"Even move to Chicago next year if that's what you want."

Cami froze, then shifted back to look in his eyes. "Why would I want to move back to Chicago?"

Vince paused and blinked as his brows lowered over his eyes. "Don't you? I mean, you know so many people there—and all of the social opportunities you're used to. We don't have that here."

She let out a full belly laugh, tipping her head back so she could let it out. "Are you crazy? I hate parties! I hate playing the social game and having to remember all of the connections between people so I can work the room and give the right image. Haven't you noticed how little I eat when we've been in things like that? They make my stomach turn. Sometimes I've actually ended up puking in the bathroom when the pressure is high. If I had my way, I'd never go back."

He leaned against the chair behind him, his eyes still narrowed in disbelief. "But you're the one they always send to work the crowd—you're really fantastic at it."

His expression was so comical, filled with total confusion. She could hardly hold back the laughter that bubbled inside her. "So it follows that it has to be the most important thing in my life?"

"But you hate it here." His brow furrowed. "Or rather, you seemed to when you first arrived. You talked like you were mad at your dad for making you come here and leave everything behind. You *were* mad about it, right?"

"Yeah, I was. I didn't like being manipulated. He'd been pushing me for months to take this job, and I hadn't wanted to be the boss, to start over in a new place. I liked the status quo despite the social obligations. But being here, meeting you—it's been the best thing that happened to me in years—maybe ever."

Vince cocked his head. "I'm the best thing that's ever happened to you?"

"Yes, you idiot. Can't you tell how much I love you?"

He grinned and pulled her close for a kiss, muttering against her mouth. "Tell me. How much, exactly?"

She slid her arms around his neck. "More than anything. More than anyone. Damn I hate it when my father's right."

He laughed. "I love you, too. I thought for sure you

wouldn't accept me, that you didn't want to stay here. If I'd known, I would have done something sooner." His lips covered hers.

Cami kissed him back, her heart threatening to explode with happiness. "It's not like you didn't make yourself clear about your feelings already," she said when his kisses trailed down her neck to her collarbone. She shivered as his lips teased her skin.

One of his arms fished in his jacket behind them while he made his way back up her neck to her ear. "So this shouldn't come as a surprise, I've waited because I had to know you loved me. I'd hoped tonight..."

Then a blue ring box appeared in his hand between them and he opened it to show off the sparkle of diamonds. "I picked this up when we were in Chicago. I knew this was the one the moment I laid eyes on it."

Cami's breath caught in her throat and she had to swallow to clear her airway. "Oh my." It was the most beautiful thing she'd ever seen. The square-cut diamond was over two carats with side stones in an antique white gold setting. If she hadn't already been ready to say yes, this would have done it.

"Marry me, Camellia DiCarlo? Stay here with me in our little Colorado town? Or let me come with you if you decide you need the city after all. I can't stand the thought of being without you. I love you so much."

The dogs whined from the back porch where he'd banished them before they'd gotten out the food. "See," he said with a chuckle, "even my dogs love you."

Tears streaked down her cheeks for the second time that day and she slid a hand behind his neck, pulling him close for a kiss. "Yes. Yes, I'll marry you, and your little town—and the two monsters you call dogs."

As they kissed, she felt him slide the ring onto her ring finger—it was a perfect fit, just like him.

NEXT IN THE DICARLO BRIDES SERIES

SEALed With Love

It isn't Sage Parker's fault that she mistakes former Navy SEAL Joel Watts as the stalker who had been sending her disturbing letters~he showed up every time she turned around. Then she learns her father hired him to protect her, and she starts to see him in a new light. When the stalker tracks Sage from LA to her new job in Colorado, she's glad to have Joel on her side. But she hadn't counted on falling in love with him~or the fact that he refused to see her as more than a client.

Joel takes his job as head of hotel security seriously, but Sage is his number one priority. He isn't sure if he buys into her precognition, but he soon finds he can't live without her. As the stalker ups the ante, Joel works to find the perp, before someone ends up dead.

Except follows:

CHAPTER 1

Sage threaded through the streaming LA crowd and wished she'd didn't have to leave for work at peak commute time. She liked people, but fighting through them wasn't exactly her idea of a party. And it was all too easy to hide in a crowd—which would be more of an advantage if she knew who she should be hiding from. *He* didn't have that problem.

She scanned the mass of people, looking for a familiar face, anyone she might have seen before, then checked her watch again. If she missed this train, she would be late. Reading her father's email had distracted her. It had been chatty and full of news about the resort he was preparing to open that fall. He put on a good front of all-is-well, but over the past few months she had been able to tell—even from their phone calls—that something was wrong. The fact that he hadn't come for his regular visit reiterated that. She'd have to check his star charts and see if she could figure it out, since he wasn't giving anything away and her unpredictable precognition hadn't been giving her any details.

A small boy weaved through the jungle of legs; a man chased him, calling out to stop. Sage shifted to the side so the boy ran into her, then she reached out and stopped him from

269

falling backward as he bounced off of her. She glanced up into the face of a frazzled man. "I believe this one belongs to you."

He hefted the tow-headed toddler into his arms. "Yes, sorry about that. He's as slippery as an eel sometimes."

Sage smiled in relief when she saw the child giggle as if it had been a good game. The boy was comfortable with the man. "No problem."

The man turned to the right, heading toward a store.

Feeling someone watching her, Sage adjusted her hemp macramé bag over one shoulder and glanced around again. Her eyes stopped on a tall man with a shaved head, mirrored sunglasses, and a light brown goatee. He oozed dark alertness, an aura of control and he was looking her direction. Her heart sped up, her breath caught, and she turned back toward the subway.

It wasn't the first time she'd seen him, or even the third or fourth. He seemed to pop up behind her all over town. There was no explanation for his repeated presence except that he was following her. Sage's hands grew sweaty as she darted farther into the crowd. If he was the one who had been stalking her, she had to get away. There was a tough wariness about him, a hardened edge that said he went after whatever he wanted, and he never gave up.

If he was the one, there may be no safe place to hide in LA safe.

She managed to slide through the train doors just before it pulled out and find a corner to stand in before her panic attack completely took over. Standing on the far end of the car, she grasped a handle until her knuckles turned white. She put her back to the wall so she could see everyone and checked for the man several times, making sure no one else was paying attention to her while she dealt with the light-headedness and nausea that often accompanied her racing heart and difficulty breathing during these attacks.

Maybe she should take up her father on the offer of a job in the Colorado resort. She couldn't keep living like this.

·

❧

While she provided reflexology treatments to the day spa's elite clientele, Sage fought the implacable image of the man in her mind. She had been at work for nearly two hours and was finally starting to feel the inner peace her job usually provided when she opened the door to leave her treatment room. Standing on the other side of the door, his fist raised to knock, was the Goliath of a man she'd seen in the street.

Her breathing stopped as terror filled her all over again. She tried to shut the door, but his hand shot out, blocking it open. "Go away." She'd meant the words to be calm and forceful, but they'd come out tight and whispery as her panic grew. What would she do? What could she do against someone his size?

"Hey, I'm sorry I scared you." His voice was a low rumble. He pulled off his mirrored sunglasses and hung them by one stem in the neck of his tight white T-shirt revealing his brown eyes. He lifted his free hand as if to reassure her that he didn't have a gun or a knife, but she seriously doubted someone that buff needed a weapon to maim or kill. "My name is Joel Watts," he said, "and your dad sent me." He handed her a business card with a private security firm's name on it.

Though she wouldn't take the card at face value, her throat unclogged a little so she could suck in some air. "My dad?" No one knew who her dad was—or almost no one. Her

271

father had been surprisingly adept at keeping their relationship a secret despite his high profile and his hundreds of phone calls and visits through the years.

"George DiCarlo," he confirmed. "He's concerned about a little trouble you've been having. Look, I'm sorry I scared you earlier today. I didn't mean to. Call him if you need to verify my story."

"Why have you been following me?" Her voice was returning to normal, though her senses were still on alert. This man was a killer; she knew it down to her core. Why would her dad send him to follow her without warning her first?

"For your protection. He's worried about your stalker." Despite the otherwise intimidating exterior, when Joel said this, his jaw softened slightly, making him seem not quite as scary.

How did her father always know what was going on in her life, even when she didn't tell him? She decided to take this hulk of a man up on his offer to check his identity. "Give me a minute, then." When he removed his hand from the door, she shut and locked it, then fished her cell phone from her capacious shoulder bag.

On the first try, the call rang several times, then went to voice mail. She hung up and called again—their agreed-upon signal that the conversation was urgent. If there was any possible way he could answer the second call, he would.

After three rings he picked up the phone. "Hey, honey, is everything all right?"

"There's a man standing outside my door. Joel Watts." *Enormous, imposing, dark.* "He said you paid him to follow me."

There was the sound of movement in the background,

272

like her father was standing and moving away from a desk or table. "I'm sorry, sweetie. He was supposed to stay in the background for now. I didn't want him to interfere or worry you."

Sage felt her pulse begin to slow more and the terror gripping her softened, though she knew from experience that it would take several more minutes to entirely dissipate. "Dad, you didn't have to hire someone."

"Yes, I did. I was worried about you when I got a report about what was going on, and you never told me about it. You can trust Joel with anything, I promise. Look, I'm sorry, I'm in a meeting right now, but I don't want to brush you off."

She smiled, knowing he'd make everyone wait for her if she needed it. "No, that was the only urgent issue. I get off at five; call me this evening when you get a chance."

"I will, and you're in good hands. I promise."

"I love you, Dad."

"I love you too, sweetheart."

Sage closed her flip phone and held it in her hand. So Joel really was working for her father. She turned to the door, unlocked and opened it. "Come in." She gestured for him to take a seat and stepped out to verify the time of her next appointment before shutting herself in the room with him.

"How tall are you, exactly?" Sage asked as she leaned back against the door, studying him.

"Six-four."

Making her feel even shorter than she had before at only five-three. "And you're a body builder?"

"Former Navy SEAL, actually." A unhurried smile spread on his face, transforming it completely. "Staying in shape is part of the job."

273

"Of course." Her dad would never settle for less than the best. Taking a deep breath, she offered him her hand. "Maybe we should start over again. I'm Sage Parker."

His hand dwarfed hers, surrounding it in hard warmth. "Joel Watts, I'm here to keep you safe."

For the first time in months, she thought she might be able to relax again.

CHAPTER 2

Joel was relieved when Sage seemed smart enough to check in with her father, and then relaxed with him—at least a little. He glanced at the comfortable-looking treatment chair and then back at Sage. "Aren't you supposed to be like a masseur or something? Can you do massage on one of those?" It seemed like an odd configuration for massage.

Sage chuckled. "I don't do that kind of massage. I specialize in reflexology." He must have looked as clueless as he felt because her lips quirked and she brushed back her unruly brown curls. "I focus on whole-body wellness through the feet."

That had him looking down at her feet. She wore hemp sandals, had her toe nails painted in bright pink, and wore silver toe rings. He'd had no clue feet could be so sexy, but they fit the package from her pixie proportions, to her wild brown curls and haunting gypsy eyes. "If you say so." Time to focus back on the reason he was there. "Though your dad had wanted me to stay incognito for a while longer, I decided it would be best if I spoke with you, especially after you spotted me. Again." She always seemed to know when he was nearby, like a sixth sense. He could usually blend into the background when he tried—especially in a crowd that size—so he was intrigued.

"I know there's a stalker," he continued. "I know you've been receiving notes and emails, but without all of the information you can give me, the chances of me catching him are minimal. The police reports only held a few details. What do you know about him—or her; it could be a woman." He thought it unlikely, but didn't want to overlook the possibility.

"Not much, but I've kept all of his notes to me. And since most of them are signed by 'your future husband,' it's unlikely the stalker is a woman." Sage folded her arms over her chest and kept her distance from him in the small room. "So how did my dad find out about it, anyway? I haven't mentioned it to him."

"The police report, though how he unearthed it, I'm not sure."

She checked her watch, something he noticed she did often, though he'd been following her for several days and she didn't seem to run late. "I only have ten minutes until my next appointment, and I have the feeling you're going to have more questions than I have time to answer right now."

Joel smiled. "I'd say that was a safe bet. How about if I meet you after you get off work? We'll eat, and I can interrogate you properly."

Sage smiled back, making something turn over in his chest. "I know just the place."

Sage watched the dismay cover Joel's face as he got a look at the offerings at her favorite restaurant—a vegetarian deli a couple of blocks from the spa where she worked. Though she didn't adhere blindly to her vegan upraising, she preferred a whole-foods approach to eating and rarely ate meat. Joel apparently had a different idea of what constituted a real meal.

She ordered a salad, he chose an egg salad sandwich—the only thing in the deli that qualified as meat in any form, and they found a table in the corner. She noticed he studied the room before sitting down, and took a seat with his back to the wall so he looked out over the deli. His eyes tracked the room and flicked back to the door every time it opened. She felt herself relax, knowing he was watching out for her. "So you're a former SEAL? How long did you do that?" she asked.

"I was in the Navy for twelve years, a SEAL for ten." He lifted the edge of his rye bread and looked at the egg filling, and though his expression was doubtful, he gamely lifted the sandwich for a bite.

"That's quite a while. Why'd you quit?" Sage speared a tomato and popped it into her mouth, studying his face. She felt better about Joel, knowing her father had sent him—her dad was no fool and would have checked his background extensively—but there was still something dark and dangerous about him. It would be a mistake to underestimate him.

"I got injured on a mission, messed up my ACL. I've been through surgery, and I'm doing great, but I'll never be at a hundred percent again." His face was calm, expressionless, but his dark brown eyes revealed his regret.

"You miss it." She didn't know much about SEALs except that they were the navy elite with advanced combat skills. She wondered if his experiences had made him dangerous, or if the inner predator had always existed and the training had merely enhanced it.

"Yeah, I miss it." He took a sip of his water and turned the conversation back to her. "So tell me about this stalker."

She washed down her salad with a drink of her tea and plunged ahead. "It started in January. At first it was just emails, then I started getting letters to my home, and deliveries of gifts to home and work. They're coming more regularly now. He seems to think we have a relationship already, but I have no idea who it is." The thought made her shiver with revulsion.

When Joel's eyes switched from cool to frigid, she was glad he was on her side.

ACKNOWLEDGEMENTS

Though writing is a solitary endeavor, I could never publish a novel without the help of many friends along the way. Thank you to Danyelle Ferguson, Rachelle Christensen, Maria Hoagland, Tamara Hart Heiner, Christine Bryant, Debbie Davis and Rebecca Blevins for taking the time to give me feedback on the editing and the story.

The internet is an awesome resource for a writer, allowing me to find information about typical weather for my fictional city, hot air ballooning and finding the perfect hotel management textbook to fill in the blanks with information my college days of working in a hotel didn't teach me. Big kudos to everyone who posts such useful information online. Seriously, you make my life so much easier!

A big, gigantic thanks to my husband who created my cover, does web work for me, reads a final time for punctuation corrections, and is just there for me all of the time. He is my staunchest cheerleader and best friend. I love you, Bill!

ABOUT THE AUTHOR

Heather Tullis has been reading romance for as long as she can remember and has been publishing in the genre since 2009. When she's not dreaming up new stories to write, she runs with the local volunteer ambulance, enjoys gardening, playing with her chickens, geese and ducks, cake decorating and working with her husband in their small business.

Learn more about her at her website at http://heathertullis.blogspot.com/ or her Facebook fan page http://www.facebook.com/HeatherTullisBooks.

Printed in Great Britain
by Amazon

84148938R00164